MW00526936

i

A Night in the Life

Steven L. Orebaugh

Pocol Press
Clifton, VA

POCOL PRESS
Published in the United States of America
by Pocol Press
6023 Pocol Drive
Clifton, VA 20124
www.pocolpress.com

Publisher's Cataloguing-in-Publication

Orebaugh, Steven L.
    A Night in the Life / Steven L. Orebaugh.
    p. cm.
    ISBN 978-1-929763-65-8

1. Emergency medicine--Fiction. 2. Hospital patients--Fiction.
3. Medical novels. I. Title.

    PS3615 .R42 Ni 2015

    813.6 --dc23   2015948322

Library of Congress Control Number: 2015948322

Acknowledgement

I would like to acknowledge the patience, encouragement and love of my wife, Jennifer, and my daughter, Olivia.

Dedication

This book is dedicated to the doctors, nurses and other staff of emergency departments everywhere, who perform critical and demanding tasks under great duress; and also to the employees of the former South Side Hospital in Pittsburgh, many of whom lost their positions or were displaced in 2009, when the hospital fell victim to the ever-shifting economic environment of American medicine.

Prologue

Gary Phillips stared blankly at the traffic light, oblivious to the change from red to green. The agitated driver behind him reminded him of his whereabouts, and he turned quickly onto the McArdle Roadway, the most direct way down into the tight mesh of riverside streets known as the Southside. The dark road sloped steeply downward, clinging to the sheer side of Mount Washington. Spindly trees, pointing awkwardly upward from the sloping earth, embraced the road on both sides as it dropped sharply along the hillside. Most of them were cloaked in a mane of grapevine that sought to choke the life out of them, and which had already left a collection of skeletal remains, festooned with the triumphant vines.

He moved along slowly, encountering no other drivers, and turned to glance into the periodic breaks between the trees, at the brightly illuminated city that lay to his left and far below. Ahead of him, further down the hill, the mouth of the Liberty tunnels, the "tubes," disgorged an endless line of cars across the adjacent bridge and into the city. The region's geography dictated a complex arrangement of roads that twisted their way through tunnels and across innumerable bridges, traversing the undulating landforms and the numerous watercourses that had carved them. Below the tunnels, the lights of the Southside flats beckoned him. A group of dark, hulking industrial structures were visible, the site of the former Duquesne brewery, a vestige of the neighborhood's industrial past. Tucked among these he could barely make out the dark roof of the South Side Hospital, his destination. From this vantage, it was difficult to see the building well, but he could make out the glow from some of the west-facing windows.

"Five minutes," he thought, "just five minutes." That was all that separated him, high on this escarpment, from the many discontented souls that he knew awaited him in the emergency department far below.

He stopped his car midway down the steep descent, and turned towards the city center, peering over the precipice. The city never looked more impressive or beckoned more bewitchingly, than it did from this lofty viewpoint. Lying just across the dark waters of the Monongahela, it was ensconced within the small

1

triangle of land at the confluence of two rivers. The narrow skyscrapers crowded each other gregariously, innumerable lights glowing. In the gentle waves on the surface of the river, he could see their reflections, a rippling mosaic that danced mysteriously before him. On the other side of the watery divide, in glittering towers of commerce, he imagined fortunes bought and sold, major financial transactions between companies and cities and nations, tendered by men in dark suits and women in fashionable business dress. He looked ahead of him at the hospital far below, dark and foreboding. His was a calling far more base; he descended each day into a morass of human misery and affliction.

The descent required little time, and he could probably have coasted all the way to the bottom, simply touching his brakes periodically. As he wound his way downward, past the yawning, blackened mouths of the Liberty Tubes, he knew he would soon find himself encompassed in darkness. It was not simply that the glow of the city's lights could no longer reach him at the base of the hill, nor that streetlights became less numerous as the boulevard ended within the warren of streets that made up the flats. Rather, there was a sense of shifting from one strata of life to another, of moving into a threatening or forbidding place. For sixteen years he'd made this short trip, almost daily, feeling his heart grow heavier with each meter of his descent. Arriving at the hospital, he would be beset by the work that awaited him, and would apply himself assiduously to people's problems great and small, to sufferings too numerous to recount.

Eventually, at shift's end, whether in the failing light of day or in the chill of dawn, he ascended back to his comfortable existence, perched atop the heights that afforded him a lofty perspective over his world.

To his right, at the top of the bluff, observation platforms protruded off of Grandview Avenue, where lovers would stand to take in the panorama, suspended over the shadowy hillside. Even now, he could make out their silhouettes, intertwined behind the railings. Briefly, he envied them their freedom on this balmy summer evening.

Drifting downgrade, he passed beneath one of the inclined railways that ferried people from the top of Mount Washington, down to the riverside. The right-of-way was outlined by rows of amber lights arrayed along the tracks. One of the classic wooden cars crossed above him, gliding as silently as a specter along its unvarying path. Two of these curious "inclines" had survived Pittsburgh's cycles of economic decay and re-vitalization, though they were now mere tourist attractions. At one time, dozens of the funiculars had provided freight and passenger service between the summits of the steep hills above the river's floodplain, and the mills and factories of the South Side. The inclined railways had once been an indispensable means of transport, a curious adaptation to the topography of the area- traversing the sheer riverside bluffs; they helped to link the communities that straddled the commanding heights to the heavy industry strewn alongside the rivers.

Shortly, Gary arrived at the bottom of the boulevard. The heights were behind him, and he made his way through the dark streets towards the hospital. He stopped at a crosswalk for a group of Friday night revelers. Already inebriated, the young men sauntered across the street against the traffic light, stumbling and laughing.

"I wonder," he mumbled, "which of them will be coming to see me before the night is over?"

They were apparently headed for a bar on the opposite corner, one of scores on the backstreets of the neighborhood. Most of these were converted from the first floor of old row houses, and marked by tiny, blackened windows, neon beer signs, and promises of discounts during happy hour or hockey games. The area had always been famous for its high bar-to-population ratio, providing the necessary services to men working tireless, round-the-clock shifts in the steel mills. More recently, they served their spirits to college and graduate students, who drifted over from Oakland on weekends to party with friends and drink too much. Many of the taverns were still haunted by stooped, wrinkled men of the older, blue-collar generation, who preferred such darkened, claustrophobic environments. The door of the establishment abruptly opened, and a volume of smoke poured out, engulfing the revelers, who disappeared into the lurid cloud.

Two blocks further along, he turned into the physician parking lot. It was empty save one car, which he recognized as that of his partner, Ken Riley. Grabbing his briefcase, he walked briskly through the small picnic area across from the front of the hospital, towards the employee entrance. Just three blocks away, he knew that Carson Street was hopping: hundreds of teens and twenty-somethings were milling tipsily along its sidewalks, moving from bar to bar to sample the drinks and check out the talent. There was the din of felicity in the air, though the hospital seemed lonely and curiously quiet this late in the evening. But around the corner, in front of the emergency entrance, there was likely to be a collection of ambulances and medics, and a few idling cars awaiting the dispositions of loved ones who were inside. Just as likely, there would be an assembly of concerned family members, who'd gathered under the eaves to smoke and share concerns.

He stood for a moment in the park, which was dark and quiet. Above the low, flat roofs of the surrounding houses, he could see the glassy skyscrapers of the Golden Triangle to the west, and to the northeast, the soaring beacon of the University of Pittsburgh's Cathedral of Learning. There had been many additions to the skyline of Pittsburgh's diminutive downtown in recent years, and he never failed to appreciate the view from his home high on the bluffs above. It wasn't his father's city, nor the one he'd grown up with. Fortune had turned its economy inside out- its blue collar attitudes persisted, but employment opportunities in manufacturing had almost completely disappeared. His own father had pushed him towards higher education, away from the searing, back-breaking work of the mills.

"And thank God," thought Gary, "for that." The loss of his father at a young age had left a profound void in the young man, and though his ideals had flickered after the older man's death, they eventually strengthened. He'd seen the dreams of friends and relatives crumble with the declension of steel in the city, as the pensions diminished and the benefits dissipated. There were no guarantees, of course, and the bright spot that health care had long represented was beginning to dim as well.

He walked across the street towards the hospital. There was music emanating from the open window of a loft apartment in what had been the malt-house of the massive brewery complex next to the hospital. It was curious, Gary thought, how life-cycles existed, in economics, in industry, and even in edifices, just as they did in biology. Below the loft, there was an art gallery, with neon lights of different colors in the window, glowing warmly in the night.

Suddenly, as he entered the hospital building, he felt it begin to shake, and sensed the earth trembling beneath his feet. The throbbing of diesel engines from a freight train speeding by on the trestle behind the hospital had once been startling to him, but was now merely one more contribution to the many background noises and sensations of the small, urban medical center. Every few minutes, a rumbling freight train on Conrail's elevated line intruded on the lives of the staff and patients, and in

4

short order left them behind, trailing only the high-pitched protests of rusted wheels and shifting rails. Some nights, Gary would take a smoke outside the department, just a few steps from the trestle.

Hurrying along, he turned into the hallway where the administration offices were located. For some reason, he was struck by the aged, neglected physical plant of the hospital. The structure was only two decades old, though it seemed much older. There was an array of time-worn, black-and-white photographs which hung on the walls in the corridor, largely ignored. The collection captured the history of the institution, and thereby, in some small way, the history of the city. Even before the town of Birmingham, later christened the "South Side," had become a part of Pittsburgh, it had been a center of the steel industry in the region. The great Jones and Laughlin steel works dominated the riverbanks of the Monongahela; it was flanked by a tight grid of modest frame row houses that marched away from the river, and up the bluffs, clinging precariously to the hillsides. Winding streets, breathtaking slopes and spindly staircases had been carrying the locals down to the mills for shifts around the clock, every day of the week for over a century.

In the heyday of steel, innumerable barges carrying raw materials had plied the muddy waters; black hulking bridges carried railcars laden with molten steel across the river, and the busy inclines shuttled freight and workers down into the smoky river valley, where towering stacks poured forth the sooty effluent of commerce. The South Side had been an important cog in the industrial machine of the greatest nation on earth.

During these frenetic, affluent years, the little hospital provided the care that kept the millworkers on the job, and their families as healthy as such an environment might allow. The stark photographs on the wall featured early ambulances; graduates of the hospital's nursing school in crisp, white hats and dresses; and class portraits of interns and residents who really did reside in the old hospital. Many of the images featured services and capabilities that had long since been dismantled, as the regional economic base had crumbled with the steel industry itself: an obstetrics unit, a variety of advanced training programs for doctors and nurses, a children's ward.

In the decades leading up to the new century, the little hospital had re-invented itself as a Medicare-dependent facility, subsisting largely on the federal monies that were disbursed to care for an aging, retired population. Gone were the great mills, now but rusting hulks overrun by weeds. Gone, too was the stature which the town had possessed as a center of the steel industry, along with the financial advantage of serving a young, insured population.

Speculation had been rampant for some time as to the likely fate of the hospital. Most believed it would simply fade away, disappearing into economic oblivion like the industries it had faithfully served. Increasingly, that was the fate of small community hospitals, which did not possess the nucleus of specialty care, sophisticated interventions and highly trained staff to maintain fiscal solvency in a world of razor-thin operating margins. Others predicted a takeover by a large hospital system, followed by conversion to some sort of specialty center-probably a rehabilitation hospital. The rumors, and the signs, had now become too widespread to ignore, and Gary had begun to discuss the future with his partners. There was no silver lining to contemplate, at least not one that was apparent to him. Closure of the facility would obviously be disastrous for those who worked there, and the neighborhood that it served. And some sort of realignment of the facility within another health care system would probably be just as traumatic for the hospital-based physicians. Such an alliance would bring a new administrator and a cadre of well-trained emergency physicians, ready to take over the staffing of the department. In short order, Gary's group would be out of a contract.

Gary paused momentarily on his way to the department. Though he'd walked past the old photos dozens of times, and seldom offered more than a passing glance, he was entranced with them on this summer evening. With a few minutes to spare, he found himself looking keenly at each, appreciating the countenances of the men and women who had proudly served the patients that had called this hospital their own for so long. He couldn't recall posing for such a photo, not recently, and perhaps not ever. As sentimental and contrived as such staged exhibitions seemed, he regretted that he'd not been recorded in similar fashion, did not occupy a place in this pantheon of providers. Throughout the Steel City, the men and women who had worked, struggled and even died in the steel mills were lauded as unsung heroes, the flesh-and-blood pillars upon which the city had been erected. But those who had aided them, provided for them, and cared for them, deserved a claim to some sort of pride as well, Gary reasoned. And on this night, he regretted that he would never be featured in this gallery, in a hallway that might soon be

6

darkened for good.

There was now little time before his shift began; he strode quickly up the stairs and into the short back hallway that led to radiology, and which provided access to his call room. He put his briefcase down, looking longingly at the bed that took up most of the diminutive space. It was neatly made; there was little reason to think he'd be able to disturb it on a Friday night. Grabbing the white coat that hung on the back of the door, with his stethoscope in one pocket and an assortment of medical instruments in the other, he headed out into the ED proper. Immediately, it was clear it had been a busy Friday evening.

11p.m.

This would be the second night shift in a string of three. He hated the night shift, had hated them since his first overnight ED shift as an intern. There was always the hope of seniority, of being guaranteed the day shifts with an occasional evening. It hadn't worked out that way; only the chief received such perks. The rest of them shared in all the spoils as well as all of the responsibilities-nights, weekends, holidays, evenings. Emergency medicine allowed for conspicuous freedom when he wasn't on duty-no pager, no cell phone calls from a busy after-hours practice. But when he was in the ED, it was intense. Pretty much what he'd signed up for. Only, he had been a whole lot younger when he made such decisions. Twenty five and brimming with confidence, he strode into his residency wide-eyed and eager for the action of emergency medicine. Lights, sirens, ambulances, helicopters, code-blues on every shift, major trauma, knife-and-gun club. But a few years later, he'd been looking for a safer haven. The University ED that had been so exciting began to seem threatening, and not in the least gratifying. Saying goodbye to that rat race, he'd found little South Side Hospital, a few miles away, and certainly on the periphery of modern medicine. Maybe even a bit beyond it, as far as modern medicine was concerned.

With nearly a decade under his belt at South Side, Gary had begun to feel more like a seasoned practitioner. He wasn't really intimidated by the job, as he once had been. But in truth, he was just weary at the prospect of another 10 or 20 years of the same. At times, he admonished himself, regarded his weariness as a crutch or an indulgence. Still, at the end of a particularly busy day or night, his head would swim with too many inputs. What, he would wonder as he lay in bed, had been left undone? Who was hiding a sign or symptom that, if he'd noted it, would have changed everything, influenced his decisions, perhaps saved a life? What had he missed? Every patient, he had begun to tell himself, was a landmine, a potentially deceptive case, with unseen hazards and unspoken clues. And it was the emergency physician's job to ferret all this out. It seemed a detective's game, sometimes. Evaluating each case, he tried to remind himself to suspect the worst, to avoid being "sucked in" by the obvious and least threatening diagnosis. It was not possible to be in this field and successfully make every diagnosis. There had been some misses, and there would be more. The object was to make sure that the misses didn't cost anybody their life. At this stage, he felt that he'd become relatively good at it, and that he could sniff out the hidden life-and-limb-threats. That didn't change the intimidation he often felt when he came on-shift.

Tonight, there were cobwebs in his brain, the residual of last night's stresses and lingering questions. Add a lousy day's sleep on top of it all. Walking into the department, Gary was gratified that, at least for the moment, there were no ambulances parked outside. He would see plenty of them, of that he was certain, but starting out without them was at least a bit auspicious.

"Hi, Karen. Good to see you again," he said to the unit secretary. Overweight and far from animated, she didn't look like the kind of person who could keep the department moving when it hit the fan, but somehow, she did. In the row of chairs behind the charting station, she had designated one of the seats as her own. It was frayed and discolored, and perhaps the metal frame was wracked a bit. But, as long as she was in that seat, things seemed to go smoothly.

"You're back, doc. You don't look very rested. Ready for a fun Friday night in the ER?" she asked as she paged through a chart, not looking up.

"Rested? I wish. I can't get any sleep during the day. No matter how tired I am." He walked back into the cluttered little room that they called the "kitchen" to find his partner, Ken Riley, scribbling away at some discharge orders. He had a stack of patient charts beside him, and grabbed another as he put the first aside.

"Hey, Gary," he said with poorly disguised glee. "It's been a busy night so far. There's a couple folks I haven't gotten to yet, back in four and seven, I think. I've got a mountain of paperwork and discharges left to do. I'll be here a while."

Riley worked hard and hated to turn patients over to the next guy. He preferred to let a patient who arrived towards the end of his shift sit in the exam room for a half hour, waiting for the next physician, if the complaint wasn't truly urgent, especially if it was likely to involve a big workup that would take a few hours. Gary didn't mind; he knew his colleague would work fervently to get the rest of the patients in the ED appropriately cared for. Some of his partners got out as fast as they could at the end of a shift, signing virtually everything out to the oncoming physician. This was truly daunting when it involved a lot of patients, especially if they were sick, and even more so if there were additional patients who hadn't been seen yet. It was a terrible way to start off a shift-behind in every possible way.

Emergency medicine was an odd sort of field. The day never really began, and it never really ended. It was always challenging to "clean things up" at the end of a shift, and one always seemed to walk in on a madhouse when the shift was starting. He often wondered what it would be like to walk into a quiet, empty office in the morning and turn the lights on to start the day.

"OK, I'll get back and see those folks. Just let me know if anything's running particularly long-I'd like to get you out of here soon."

It was a salute to the intense ten hours that the other had just spent in the cramped patient rooms and the claustrophobic kitchen, or behind the charting desk-one encounter after the next, with the constant pressure to keep up, see the new ones, check the other ones, and get them admitted or discharged as fast as possible.

Riley waved off this kindness with a sweeping gesture.

"No problem. I've got this stuff."

Gary went out to inspect the chart rack. There were two of the familiar blue metal tablets there, a form from registration on top of each that described the patient's information as well as a place for physician orders. On the back was an area for nurse's notes and vital signs. Sometimes, in his haste to get back to see the patient, he'd forget to look at these, and he'd more than once learned his lesson. What the triage nurse elicited from the patient might or might not correspond to what he learned from that person back in the exam room, but it was often valuable. The patient who was willing to divulge important, if subtle, symptoms with a soft-spoken nurse in the quiet of the triage office might not feel the same way when the physician appeared and asked what

9

was wrong. He knew, too, that when things were busy, he himself could take on a very brusque, officious manner, which intimidated some patients. He had learned to try to break through that, to sit down and at least briefly touch a patient. This could open up lines of communication that many minutes of mere questioning could not. As a young doc, he hadn't grasped the importance of physical contact to show caring-it had been simple and quick: listen to the heart and lungs, then poke at the painful part. That approach didn't win many hearts.

Picking up the first chart, he felt the familiar vigor that always coursed through him as he began a shift-shedding his reservations and shelving his feelings of fatigue, it was now "go time." The triage note described a young boy who'd injured his arm skateboarding.

He looked up at the anxious, waiting faces in the series of chairs besides the triage room. There was nothing else to call the area, except "the chairs," where overflow patients with minor complaints were relegated to wait while the staff walked briskly past them en route to the actual exam rooms to see the more urgent players. The boy, a sullen adolescent, sat mutely with his father, who looked more than a little displeased.

"Mr. McElroy? And Peter? What happened to your arm?"

Peter was tall and skinny, all angles in ripped jeans and a black concert t-shirt. He slouched in the time-honored teenaged fashion, and let his father do the talking. The relationship between the two seemed a bit strained, and Gary wasn't sure if this was due to the lateness of the hour, the length of the wait, or parental disapproval of the manner in which the boy had injured himself.

"Peter fell off his skateboard," the father grumbled, looking askance his son with a frown firmly embedded in his face.

"I didn't fall," the son corrected, looking ahead at nothing in particular. "Some asshole left a bottle on the sidewalk-I had to try to get around it and the board went out from under me."

His father looked at him more directly.

"Right. Then you fell. That's what I said."

The boy shook his head and muttered to himself. His long hair had fallen into his eyes, and he seemed to hide behind the bangs, frustrated with his father's inability to accept his explanation.

"Ok-let me look at your films, and we can try to get you out of here," the physician offered. He knew he would have to address the wait, which had apparently been lengthy. He braced for the anger that he knew would surface.

10

"We've been here for three hours!" the man spit through his clenched teeth, turning his intense, blue eyed gaze upon Gary.

The emergency physician silently cursed his luck. Arriving at the tail end of a busy evening shift often meant seeing a handful of really upset people, who'd patiently waited their turn, but who then simply had to unload on somebody. It was usually the night doc, right after he walked in the door. This was exactly why Gary liked to see every patient, or nearly every one of them, at the end of his evening shifts, before the night doctor came in. Any attention from a physician, even just a brief interview, gave patients the sense that something was happening. There was a lot of customer service involved in the ED, something he'd never envisioned when he was in training. Then again, academic hospitals in the inner-city seldom promoted service or efficiency-it was a different mindset altogether. Waiting on people and stroking them wasn't his forte, but he had learned over the course of his years of experience to be more sympathetic. It was easy to say "I wasn't here until a few minutes ago," or, "I just came on." But people didn't want to hear that. They wanted some recognition that their time was valuable. His naturally defensive posture had, over the years, given way to an ability to apologize on behalf of the hospital, and not feel responsible. Sometimes, when people were especially belligerent, he had a hard time adopting that stance. The feelings would come welling up within him, and he wanted to scream: "I'm a physician. I work very hard. I don't make people wait any longer than necessary. Give me a break." At such times, he had to brace himself, ignore his own ignominy, and utter the kindest apology he could muster. Sincerity included.

"I'm sorry sir, that you had to wait so long."

The man took a deep breath, remained silent, and handed him the films. He was still overtly angry, but Gary felt the tension ease a bit. He took the envelope and walked down the hallway to the view box. He almost always examined patients before looking at films, but he wanted to give the two the appearance that things were happening more rapidly. Slapping the films onto the glowing, opaque white box, he eyed the X-rays carefully. The boy's physes, or growth plates, were not closed. As tall as he was, he still had some growing to do. Nothing looked fractured or out of alignment. He traced the cortices about the distal radius and ulna, and looked at the wrist bones as well, asking himself if all eight of them were where they belonged. It looked as though there was some soft tissue swelling about the wrist. That was worrisome, but could certainly be indicative of a mere contusion or a ligament

11

sprain. It was presumptive to tell a patient with open physes that he had a sprain, especially if he was tender over the growth plate. Kids, even big ones, were susceptible to fracture through the physis, which, when mild, could leave virtually no trace on the X-ray.

The consequences included deformity and growth retardation of the involved bone. The safe thing to do was to splint the wrist and forearm, and have the young man follow with an orthopedist. If the tenderness and swelling resolved in a week or so, the surgeon would be satisfied that the injury was purely related to the soft tissue, and the splint could be discarded. It was simply impossible to know on first examination, so a lot of children ended up with splints.

He pulled the films down demonstratively, turned and headed straight for the injured boy, avoiding any eye contact or communication that might detain him.

"Can I examine your arm?" he asked Peter, gently.

The lanky youth extended his right arm, reluctantly.

"Hmmm. Is this tender? It does seem swollen and red."

"Uhhh, yeah, that hurts," he admitted.

"Can you bend the wrist, back and forth, like this?"

He did as he was told, wincing a bit. Gary nodded, and moved his fingers up and down the arm and onto the hand, checking the proximal and distal joints. Everything was intact, in terms of function. The soreness and pain were most likely due to direct trauma over the distal wrist, which was somewhat abraded. He explained that the films were normal, but that a growth plate fracture would not show up at this early stage.

"We'll put it in a splint, and a sling. I want you to keep it iced and elevated as much as possible."

"OK, doc," the father commented. His manner was much gentler, and he seemed apologetic.

Gary paused for a moment and looked at the man. He was every construction worker he'd ever met: coarse, proud, calloused, contentious, respectful until he felt he'd been disrespected. He was a bit afraid of these men-he couldn't always control the circumstances that infuriated them. But he felt a twinge of remorse when he considered their lot-their work appeared then disappeared, briefly paid well then dried up, provided for them then left them hanging. Pittsburgh was bursting with them-young men, eager to work, not interested in bookish pursuits but happy to throw their backs into it for a good day's wage. They became middle aged, broken down, disillusioned with disappearing prospects- but by that point so many had become accountable for wives, homes, big pickups trucks, and kids. When they showed up as patients, and he asked them what they did, the answer was so often "construction, doc...but I haven't worked in a few months." These were the men, legions of them, who were raised by proud fathers to work in the mills that had closed and now lay in rusted ruins throughout the river valleys that radiated like spokes from the center of the city.

The father's softening demeanor was precisely what the physician had hoped for. He shook hands with both of them, scribbled some orders for the splint, and a prescription for ibuprofen, to help the pain and inflammation.

"Do you think Motrin will be all right for the pain?" he asked the pair.

"Oh yeah, he's tough as nails. Helps me on the job in summers, and that. Don'tcha, Pete?"

The man elbowed his son, and the boy sheepishly nodded, as though he would not have wanted anyone else to know this.

"Carol, can you make this young man a splint for the distal radius, just to keep it in neutral position?" Gary called out to a middle-aged lady in green scrubs, who happened to be walking by.

"OK, doc. Not a pre-made one, but a plaster one?" she asked, eyeing the boy's arm.

Carol was the night aide. She was very kind to patients, as well as helpful to doctors. And respectful to everyone. She didn't have a great deal of medical knowledge but she made up for it with her optimism and her energy. With dark hair and large, dark eyes, she moved inconspicuously from bedside to bedside, appearing just as needed. Her face bore a timeworn appearance that made it hard to guess her age-she was neither old nor young, she was just there. The aides made very little for their hard work; there wasn't a trace of glamour in the position. For a lot of them, the attitude matched the sophistication of the job description. Carol paid no heed to the station that this job placed her in-she came to the situation with humility and pride. Her speech was coarse, and laden with the heavy South Side accent that was so common among those who'd been reared in that area. Like many who worked in the hospital, she was South Side born and raised, and the daughter of a "mill hunkie." In her demeanor there was a sort of dogged earnestness. Rarely did enthusiasm manifest itself in her features, but she persevered until whatever was required was accomplished. No questions, just attentiveness to her duties. Sort of a medical Marine. Gary wished all of the aides were so industrious, and was grateful when he found himself on a shift with her. When the docs and nurses were too busy to lavish attention on a patient with a minor illness or injury, Carol often stepped in. She was singularly responsible for preventing a lot of complaints, Gary figured.

"Yeah," he said, sending her a curt smile, "a plaster splint. Take him back to the cast room and put it on, if you would."

Gary grabbed the remaining chart in the box and headed back to room 6. The ED was a claustrophobic affair, long and narrow, bisected by a long desk with high sides covered in a light gray laminate at which the staff periodically sat, creating reports and wading through the necessary paperwork. Off of the long corridor were 9 cramped exam and treatment rooms, the first two a bit more spacious for dealing with the most serious cases. The last one, referred to as the "cast room," was chock full of orthopedic supplies; room 7 was called the "Gyn room" because it had a table with stirrups for pelvic exams. As the corridor proceeded away from the desk and the two big trauma rooms directly in front of it, it narrowed, like a bizarre funnel that channeled the ED physician deep into the secret and sometimes sordid lives of the clientele.

On the other side of the desk, a paired set of sliding glass doors opened onto a carport and thence into the diminutive ED parking lot. The medics used the ambulance doors to bring the sicker patients in, while the "walking wounded," who called the ambulances primarily for a ride to the hospital, were made to sign in out in front, at the triage desk in the waiting room.

When not fronted by an idling ambulance rig bringing a patient, the doors afforded a view of a high black wall, hewn of some type of porous local sandstone, and preserved over the decades by thick layers of soot that shielded the soft rock from the elements. Upon this perch, the elevated Conrail line hosted thunderous freights that shook the entire hospital with unsettling regularity.

It wasn't one of the city's busiest ER's, Gary reflected, and he silently thanked God for that. The staffing configuration was right at the limit of acceptable for the 15,000 patients that they registered each year. On many evening shifts he'd yearned to have a second physician working in tandem with him, someone who could really move the patients in and out. Instead, it had been decided that staffing should be comprised of a single physician around the clock, paired with a physician assistant or nurse practitioner from 11a.m. to 9p.m. The ten hours of double coverage were helpful, and certainly preferable to having only one provider, but the physician extenders were required to present the cases to the emergency physician, who was busily seeing patients himself. That meant he might not get around to actually hearing about the cases that the extender had seen for a half hour or longer. Meanwhile, the PA or NP had to stand around and wait for the magic moment when the doc was free to hear about the case. Most of the complaints that they saw were pretty standard stuff: colds, twisted ankles, rashes, contusions, minor lacerations. But this situation severely restricted the efficiency of the extender, and the department in general. It simply took too long to get patients through the ED. What resulted were long waits, particularly for those with minor illnesses and injuries, and really angry patients. Just a bit busier, Gary figured, and the staffing pattern would collapse like a house of cards. It would simply be untenable. Then again, a few thousand more patients might make the addition of the second doc financially reasonable.

Entering the tiny exam room, he greeted the waiting patient.

"Hello Mr. Kitwicki," he announced to an older man who was lying in the bed with his sheet pulled up around him. "What can I do for you tonight?"

Older men usually waited quietly while their wives related their symptoms and medical history. This gentleman was no exception. With gray skin and pale lips, the diminutive, balding man looked miserable. The woman with him, presumably the missus, was a mere bird of a lady, perhaps five feet tall and not likely to weigh a hundred pounds. She had an energetic, unsettled manner that made Gary feel a bit uneasy. Fielding virtually all the physician's questions, she seldom allowed her husband to volunteer an answer. However, she was a capable historian, and very knowledgeable about his conditions.

"Well, doctor," she began, looking at Gary with disarming blue eyes, "He's been having this dizziness. It comes in waves, then he has terrible nausea and throws up."

There was a plastic kidney-shaped emesis basin by the man's head, with some bilious-looking fluid inside. A thin string of saliva still connected his lower lip to the basin. His eyes were closed, and his face was contorted in a tight grimace, as though whatever had forced him to throw up in the basin had him in its malevolent grip again.

"When he's dizzy, he can't move," the woman explained. "He has to hold his head in a certain position. He's been doing this all day. I can't even keep broth in him."

15

At this the man turned onto his side and began retching forcefully. The guttural gagging sound he made spilled out into the hallway, resounding through the entire department. Gary felt a little queasy himself as he listened to the man. He went to his side and put a hand on his shoulder, which moved up and down spasmodically with each dry heave the man endured.

"Sir, let's get an IV started so we can give you some fluid and some medication to try to stop this dizziness. You're probably pretty dehydrated."

"Nurse!" he called out, to no one in particular, "Who's on tonight, anyway? Could someone give me a hand and start an IV in here, please?"

Apparently, the nurses were all busy, as no one responded. He decided to do a quick exam and then get the orders written. The man would probably end up staying as an inpatient, unless he dramatically improved in the ED. Gary had suffered from similar bouts of vertigo himself, usually in tandem with upper respiratory infections. It gave him real satisfaction to relate to patients when he'd had problems similar to theirs; somehow it made him feel more authentic as a physician.

"Mr. Kitwicki, I've had these kinds of symptoms myself. It's usually due to an inner ear infection, and I can treat it with some medication. I know you're miserable, but with some fluids we can get you feeling better."

"But Doctor, could it be something serious?" asked the man's wife as the physician struggled to perform a neurologic exam, with the man lying on his side, periodically heaving. She was clearly very worried.

"Well, it can be, but most of these types of episodes are not, they're due to a virus or benign positional vertigo. He doesn't seem to have any evidence of nervous system dysfunction that would point to a stroke or brain tumor. Has he had any cold symptoms lately? That would make me lean more towards the inner ear infection." Under the circumstances, Gary tried to be as reassuring as he could.

She paused, and recollected "He had a cough and a bit of a runny nose earlier in the week. I was sick with some kind of flu last week, myself."

The physician turned and regarded her.

"That's a pretty common story, when people come in with sudden attacks of vertigo like this. I really don't think we need to worry about stroke with this sort of presentation."

Eying the listless man, he went through the "rule out" list in

16

his head: nothing here to suggest a stroke, too abrupt for a brain tumor, no evidence of a systemic or localized infection, nothing that looked like lightheadedness from low blood pressure as opposed to a true vertigo, no disturbance of hearing to support a more chronic process like Meniere's disease. It was always important to consider the really scary things in old people before settling on a benign diagnosis-they just had a tendency to hide so many important disease processes.

"We'll get the IV started and get him some medication. I think he'll feel better in a short while, maybe even good enough to go home. The drugs will probably make him sleepy, though."

The man rocked back and forth, clutching the emesis basin. He seemed to be done puking for the moment, so Gary took the basin and dumped the liquid, which had become rather clear, into the sink, rinsing it out. He handed it back to the man, who uttered a pathetic "thank you" in a weak voice.

"Doctor?" he asked, turning his head to look at the emergency physician.

"Yes sir?"

"If there's any way I can go home, please work on that. I don't want to stay."

His wife frowned intently at him, and looked back to Gary. She disregarded his statement, apparently for his own good.

"Do whatever you need to do, doctor. I'll make sure he's a good patient."

He turned to leave, and heard her rebuking her husband behind him. No doubt, the physician thought, who is in charge in that household.

As he exited the room, Carol crossed his path, leading a very distressed young man across the along the dim corridor. His face was contorted, his arms held out in front of him stiffly, his gait unsteady. The man's head was carried at a very odd angle.

"Hmmm, looks like a dystonic reaction. Easy to recognize, easy to treat," Gary said to himself.

The triage nurse followed the patient into the room, hurriedly scribbling her note.

"What's up Margie?" he asked, joining the procession.

"This is Michael. He was here last evening for nausea and vomiting, got some IV fluids and Phenergan, and was discharged. Now he says he can't control his arms and legs, and his neck is in some sort of spasm. He can't even speak without slurring. It's like he's lost control of his muscles, or something."

Gary had heard this story many times before. The very

17

appearance of the patient, struggling to carry out the simplest tasks, was virtually quite specific to this entity. Once recognized, he mused, it's never forgotten.

"Margie-you got it. That's exactly what's going on," he commented, helping the aide get the young man into the bed, almost against his will, as he struggled to control his limbs. Margie was a new nurse, recently graduated from college, having just completed her clinical rotations. She'd probably read about this sort of problem, but never actually seen it. She was filled with the energy that new grads always seemed to have, and was wonderfully personable. Over time, the pressures and demands of the ED could quench such enthusiasm in a nurse, or a medical student. For now, it was simply a pleasure to see the verve with which she approached every patient.

He called out to the nursing station, "Karen, could you ask one of the nurses out there to draw up some Benadryl, and get some IV supplies?"

Then, turning back to the triage nurse, whose countenance reflected her puzzlement, he said, "What does this make you think of?"

Gary had liked her immediately when she was hired. He could see she loved to learn, and that, for him, was a great inducement to spend some of his time teaching.

"I think it's like some kind of muscle disorder. He's lost control, or lost his coordination, I think." She held the young man's hand, tightly, helping him to control himself and offering a sympathetic touch at the same time.

The patient, frustrated and anxious, tried to speak, but what came out was garbled. It was clear that he was capable of forming thoughts and expressing them, but his control of motor function was badly disordered. He drooled a bit, and it appeared that even swallowing was an effort. He was frightened, and squeezed the nurse's hand with uncontrollable vigor. Carol was busy trying to obtain vital signs, a real challenge with the patient's inability to cooperate. She repeatedly cycled the blood pressure cuff, only to watch the determination fail because of the incessant motion of his arms.

"Well, right," he explained to the nurse, impassively. "Disordered muscular control, of acute onset, in a young, otherwise healthy patient-what does that make you think of?"

She furrowed her brow, and thought this over.

"I don't exactly know, Doctor. Maybe a toxin or poison of some type?"

"Yes-you're thinking along the right lines, now."

The patient's expression became even more terrified, if that was possible. By this time, Lizzie, one of the two night nurses, had waddled in and begun searching for a site to place the IV.

"OK," she said, as she slid the catheter home, "now who gets the Benadryl-the patient, or Margie?"

Lizzie didn't smile very much, but she did enjoy chiding the younger nurses, and sometimes brandished her own experiences in a heady way.

Margie looked pained, and Gary chuckled. The patient, for his part, was not enjoying their witty banter.

"Twenty-five milligrams, IV, ought to do it, Lizzie," he said.

"Right," he continued, turning back to Margie, "it's a toxin. And the Benadryl is an antidote-but to what?"

"Hmmm, the Phenergan?" she guessed, not really making the connection.

"Exactly," he coaxed, "and how does such a drug cause this kind of movement disorder?"

She looked blankly at him, awaiting the answer.

"They are anti-dopaminergic in the central nervous system. This is a dystonic reaction. Margie, once you've seen this, you'll never forget it. Nothing else-not a stroke, not a seizure, not chorea-nothing else looks quite like this. My residency director used to call this an 'Aunt Minnie.' You might not be able to describe your aunt Minnie exactly, but you would always know her when you saw her...and nobody else looks quite like her."

The triage nurse raised her eyebrows, apparently trying to imagine what his Aunt Minnie actually looked like, as Lizzie hustled out of the room, intent upon another task. The atmosphere in the room had lightened remarkably. The patient, who now appeared to have regained his coordination, was lying comfortably on the bed, and was evidently very relieved. The contortions on his face were gone, and his countenance had softened.

"What the hell was that?" he asked, genuinely astonished at what had happened to him.

Gary grabbed the stool that was in the room, sitting down in front of the stretcher.

"Michael, that was a reaction to the nausea medication that you took. It can cause a problem with how your nerves direct your muscles. It feels terrible, but it's not dangerous."

The young man's eyes opened widely.

"Terrible-yeah, right. I thought I was going to die. I couldn't even swallow a sip of water. You guys should warn people about that!"

"Well, we do. Did you read the discharge instructions?"

"You mean all that paperwork you sent me home with? Of course not. But if I'd known..."

"Honestly, Michael, we wouldn't send all that stuff out with you if it wasn't important."

"Now I know," he acquiesced. "From now on, I read the discharge papers. What do I do now? How do I keep this from happening again?"

"Do you still have the nausea?"

"No, not really. I feel OK."

"Well, first of all, no more Phenergan. Second, let's keep you on the Benadryl until tomorrow, that should prevent any relapse. After that you'll be fine. I'll see to your paperwork, and we'll get you out of here. Let me go over you quick, just to make sure things are OK."

He grabbed the boy's paperwork and scribbled the results of a cursory physical exam. He then proceeded to ask a series of unrelated questions, about drug and alcohol abuse, sexual habits, and various other body systems that were clearly not affected by the episode.

"Why all the questions? I thought you said this was, like, open-and-shut?" the boy asked, interested but not annoyed.

"Believe it or not, to send a bill to an insurance company, we have to address a variety of questions in different areas, to prove that the history and exam were suitably comprehensive. Otherwise, we won't get paid. They call it 'E and M' coding. It's a little strange-we used to just treat what was wrong with you. Medicine is different now. Administrators and insurance companies want us to look at the whole patient, not just the part that hurts. Actually, it makes a lot of sense, but it probably doesn't make a whole lot of difference here in the ER. There's just not a lot of time for health counseling. "

"Well, to be honest, I don't exactly have any insurance. I'm between jobs right now."

"It doesn't much matter, then. We don't have to worry about anyone rejecting the bill."

"I might have to pay it off over time, I mean, things are bad right now. I'm hoping they'll call me back to work soon."

"It's OK. People who can't pay often don't pay. We're not going to refuse you care in the future. But hospitals can be pretty persistent. They may pester you until you come see them to set up a payment plan, or something. And, if you don't respond at all, after a few bills, they may get a collection agency involved. So give the billing office a call once you get the bill in the mail."

He tried to soften the blow as much as possible. The kid had no money, probably wouldn't send a dime, and might end up getting blacklisted on some credit report. Or worse, some collection agency drone might hassle him endlessly. It was becoming the new normal: young people with no major health problems, working at service jobs, or unemployed, barely making ends meet- and they didn't see the wisdom of paying for health insurance. When something did finally go wrong, they were completely unprepared to deal with the costs.

"So, what do you do, you know, when there's work?" Gary asked, expecting the boy to say something about construction or contracting.

"I'm a bicycle courier-we can get stuff across this town faster than any van or taxi."

"Yeah, I've seen some couriers out there pushing it through the traffic. Seems like a tough job."

"It's not so bad, down here in the flats, or going across the Tenth Street Bridge into town. But when you have to go up the slopes, or ride up onto Mount Washington, that's different-they get to ya, those hills."

"People get pretty steamed at you guys, darting in and out..." Gary grinned at the youth, imagining him slicing between moving cars, riding up the right side of the cars at the red lights, veering onto the sidewalks when necessary.

Michael looked wistful. "Well, yeah. But if we follow every little rule, we take as long to get there as everyone else does. Some people get pretty mad and act like jag offs. One guy chased me in his car, to the bottom of that stairway here on 18th street, that long one that goes up above the railroad track."

He gestured generally in the direction of the railroad embankment.

"I threw my bike on my back and ran like anything. I looked back and seen him following me like a bat outa hell up them steps-I thought he was gonna kill me."

"What happened?"

"This happened," he said, pointing to a scar on his temple. "The guy decked me, knocked me halfway down the steps, left me laying there. Ruined my bike, then took off. Said I cut him off. I don't think I did, he was just a jag off."

"So how much will it be?" he asked after a moment, looking

expectantly at Gary.

"What?"

"You know, the ER visits. Two in just a couple days!"

The physician frowned, hoping to avoid a long discussion about billing.

"Michael, I really don't know. I bet it's a few hundred bucks. Depends on what all they did last night and how long you were here. The ladies out front, in registration, could tell you more. It's embarrassing for me to admit this, but coding and billing are like a medical specialty all on their own. I know what I get paid to work here per hour, and that's pretty much where my knowledge of the finances end."

The young man nodded thoughtfully, probably wondering how he would cope with this new expense that he obviously hadn't planned for.

"But stay tuned," Gary added. "I think by about a decade from now, everyone in this country will have some sort of national insurance. We'll have to pay for it with more taxes, of course. But it's going to happen, I'm sure of it."

Michael sat up straighter on the cart. "Well, it can't happen too soon for me."

"I think a lot of people feel that way. We'll be in for a lot of changes, I think."

Lizzie stuck her head in, eyeing the two of them. She didn't approve of idle chatter, and probably had decided that Gary had gone on long enough.

"Doctor, we just got a chest pain in room 2."

Innervated, the physician turned his head toward the boy as he briskly exited the room.

"I'll get these discharge instructions ready-don't forget to read them!"

The young man smiled sheepishly as he watched the physician leave.

"Course not, Doc."

Gary reflected on the exchange as he hurried up the narrow corridor. "What a nice kid," he thought. That sort of interaction was immensely satisfying, probably as much as anything he did. A clear diagnosis. A patient in distress, easily and effectively managed. Teaching a young healthcare worker at the bedside. A bit of patient education. Even a chance to chat before he left the room, without pressure to get on to the next. Of course, it was short-lived, and there was another patient to see in no time. But such encounters justified his existence, and gave him a real feeling

22

of worth.

Lizzie was standing in the doorway of room two, looking in at the patient, and waving at him.

"Here, doctor Phillips," she called.

He rolled his eyes as he approached, then checked himself, hoping she would not see. Did she think somehow that he could not remember where the room was? Sometimes, she displayed an imperious side to her nature that annoyed him. But she was a good, experienced nurse, who, he conceded, sometimes took more time to get things done than he would have liked. When things were hopping, he stressed her with requests, he knew, but the department had to run. She sometimes spent a little too much time counseling patients. Maybe scolding would be a better term- she wasn't the least bit reticent to read patients the riot act for careless or self-defeating behaviors that landed them in the ER.

He approached the bedside to find a twenty-something man, clutching his chest.

"Right here, doc, right in the center," the man noted, pointing to his breastbone.

He was tall and athletic-appearing, with wavy brown hair that came almost to his shoulders, and goatee. His face was ruddy and creased, as though he spent most of his time outside. There were interesting tattoos all over the visible parts of his body-arms, shoulders, top of the chest, ankles. Mostly of a fantasy motif, the physician noted. They appeared to tell some sort of a story as one's eyes moved from one to another, but Gary didn't have the time to look at them all.

"When did this all start?" he asked, jotting some notes.

To his satisfaction, the nursing staff and techs had already started an IV, drawn blood for lab tests, taken the initial vital signs, placed the monitors. Sometimes this was all done by the time he got to the bedside, sometimes not. It certainly moved things along if such tasks were completed early, and they were virtually always necessary. It wasn't only efficiency that was in play. If there was a sudden change in vital signs, or in the cardiac rate and rhythm, it was imperative that an IV route was available for fluid or medications. The delay in obtaining immediate access could be costly, even life-threatening.

He helped the man put his shirt in a "personal effects" bag, while he quickly examined his heart and lungs. These seemed pretty normal, as did the exam of his ears and throat. The belly was soft and not tender. The man's chest wall, on the other hand, was quite tender over the breast bone, or sternum, especially

23

where the ribs connected to it on the left side.

"Yeah, right there," the man grunted when Phillips pressed. He had a small, pointed goatee of close-cropped dark hair, and wore a plethora of jewelry.

"When did it start up, this pain?"

"I think about a half hour ago. It was really intense."

"Does it get worse when you breathe, or move?"

"Yeah-when I breathe in real deep, or when I twist like this," he said, leaning forward in the bed.

"Karen, I need a chest X-ray on this man," he called over his shoulder, "and an EKG. Did anybody call for EKG?"

"Both ordered already," Karen confirmed, matter-of-factly.

Gary pondered this. Pain with breathing was usually considered pleuritic- related to the lungs or pleura. But other types of pain could cause this, too, even chest wall pain or cardiac pain. It was unlikely that this young man would have pain related to his heart, unless he had some sort of cardiac in his heart, or was using illicit drugs.

"Are you pretty healthy, other than this? Do you smoke? Any drugs, either IV or smoked or pills? Was there any trauma to your chest? Do you feel short of breath?" The physician poured out a fusillade of questions, eyeing the monitors intently.

The man paused and then answered in turn. His speech came out in short, staccato bursts, as though it literally hurt to talk.

"Yeah, I guess I'm healthy. I smoke about a half-pack. I do some reefer once in a while when I'm partyin'. I don't really feel short of breath, though. It just hurts to breathe."

"No other drugs-no cocaine?"

"Naw. I don't do that stuff. Just a little weed."

"That's good. Cocaine is bad news. Marijuana is bad enough, though."

"No meds or allergies?"

"No, doc, I'm never at the doctor's office."

A tech came in with an EKG machine and began hooking up the leads. As he placed each of the tabs on the skin in the appropriate places, he commented on the tattoos at the site.

"Cool. And what's this one?" he asked repeatedly moving from one work of body art to the next. The patient narrated a sequence of events from the tattoos on his legs to those on his abdomen, shoulders, back arms and neck. Apparently, they were all from a futuristic comic book series.

"Your tattoo guy must be quite an artist," the tech said,

24

admiringly. Gary hadn't worked with him before, but noticed he had quite a series of tattoos on his arms and neck as well, along with jewelry configured in odd places on his eyebrows, lips, tongue and upper ear. Kindred spirits, the physician observed, briefly amused. The fact that the two were exchanging pleasantries about body art made him feel better. Pain from serious diagnoses, such a pulmonary embolism or cardiac disease, was unlikely to leave the man feeling so sociable. It was nothing to hang his hat on, of course, but it did mitigate somewhat against the life-threats. He guessed that the chest film and EKG would be normal, and that he'd be left with 'chest wall pain' or 'costocondritis' as the probable diagnosis. He had seen pneumothorax, a so-called 'popped lung,' present this way a couple of times, but the vast majority of such young, otherwise healthy patients would have inflammation of the bones, muscles or cartilages of the chest cage as the cause of their chest pain. Mysterious in its origin, but benign, and easy enough to treat. A shot of ketorolac, an anti-inflammatory, ought to be adequate to make the man feel better. This wouldn't obscure any other diagnoses, and was safe in a single dose, though a course of it could irritate the stomach.

He called to Lizzie, asking for the injection, and scrutinized the EKG. It was remarkable for some changes in the anterior leads suggestive of either a cardiac event, or else a muscular, thin-walled male. The latter made much more sense in this setting. By this time the radiology tech had lumbered in with the big, portable machine and was putting the patient into a sitting position, in order to get the plate behind him for the film.

"I guess I ought to get a toxicology screen, too," he thought aloud, though no one was within earshot. It would likely be positive for marijuana, and perhaps for other substances, too, which might or might not relate to the case. But, as he had learned, people who used illicit drugs frequently didn't tell the whole truth. There was reason enough to sample his urine.

"Hey, Karen, add a tox screen, will you?"

"Sure doc, anything for you," she called back, cheerily.

Gary's predecessor, working fervently to tie everything together so he could leave, had just asked her to put in a few more orders for his patients, as well. Karen never got flustered, though, no matter how many tasks were laid at her feet. She just plowed through them and kept paddling till she found herself upstream the water again. He admired her impassiveness, her steadiness in the face of pressure. And her visage never changed-she simply

25

wore an expression of bemused determination on her round, oily face.

He retreated to the nursing station in the center of the ED, intent on taking inventory. His colleague was waiting for him, with a pair of charts in his hand.

"You need to sign some stuff out?" Gary asked, putting his hand on the man's shoulder. He knew that the other been hustling for 10 hours, likely with little break or relief. The ED was an intense, energetic, draining atmosphere. You might rush around seeing patients for five hours before you even realized you had to go to the bathroom. The stress that built up inside sometimes wasn't evident, though, until you tried to leave. And suddenly you found various loose ends that hadn't been tied up, and wouldn't be for another 30 or 60 or 90 minutes. Then you felt the burden, the fatigue, and even the shame of having to sign out some elements of patient care to the next guy. Shame because you'd been the one who examined the patient and then discussed his care with him, and shame because usually the guy coming on was hit with a barrage of new patients that just happened to build up around the time that shifts changed. Nurses and doctors were a bit reluctant to grab those charts in the few minutes before the shift ended, as long as they weren't bona fide emergencies. It was a little irritating to Gary to have patients signed out to him, especially when he'd been assured that it would all be "taken care of."

But he understood. It was getting late; the things that were signed out were usually not going to be resolved for quite a while.

"Thanks, Gary. They're simple cases, and I'll have everything ready to go so that you can dispo them when the labs come back. First, I have a 20 year old with abdominal pain in room 3. I think it's gastritis, and we gave him a 'GI cocktail' with pretty good results. No vomiting, minimal epigastric tenderness. He's a healthy guy who drank a 12 pack last night. His labs were never drawn, even though I wrote for them two and a half hours ago. Typical lab oversight. He's awaiting a set of liver functions, a hemoglobin and some pancreatic enzymes. The good news is that he's definitely more comfortable now. And, fortunately, or unfortunately, they just drew the blood."

Gary recognized the problem, the presentation, the solution. Pretty common among the young people who inhabited this tavern-filled corner of the city. It would be simple to wrap things up and "disposition" the man back home, with a prescription for meds for his stomach for a couple of weeks, and a

26

recommendation to avoid alcohol for a good while. He didn't really expect compliance, but at least the guy was feeling better for the moment. Probably, he should be scoped, just to rule out anything sinister in his upper GI tract-even young people could get esophageal or stomach cancers. This was especially true if they abused alcohol and smoked, like so many of the weekend crowd that piled in. Likely, the guy would recover, would never follow up with the PCP that they referred him to, and of course would not get a referral to a GI specialist to get the scope. At any rate, Gary would make the suggestion in the discharge orders.

"OK, fine. What else?"

"Lady with a UTI. Probably pyelonephritis. She presented with fever and back pain. She's had a liter of fluid and three grams of IV Unasyn. Still having shaking chills. The urine showed a bunch of white cells and bacteria, and her white count was 16,000."

"What does she need?"

"Well, she's still having chills, like I said. She's nauseated, too. She just doesn't look good. I called her PCP and talked to him about admission. He's not convinced, asked that we continue the fluids, give her some Phenergan or Zofran for the nausea, and see if we can turn her around. She's had Tylenol for the fever, we've drawn blood and urine cultures..."

"Why Unasyn?"

"That's the antibiotic that her PCP wanted...his name's Abami. Cross-covering tonight."

"I see. Well, I'm happy to watch over her. Does she know she may not go home?"

"Yeah. I think she and the husband would prefer to stay."

"But, the cross-cover PCP who doesn't know the patient doesn't want to admit her, and we get the 'credit' for the decision, right?"

"You guessed it. I told him if she fails, we're going to admit, and I already put a basic set of admission orders on the chart."

"I can deal with that. Thanks for taking care of all this stuff. Can we go to the bedside and meet this lady, in case things start looking rosy and I have to send her home against her will?"

Gary nodded towards the corridor.

"Oh, yeah" he said, standing up abruptly, "let's go."

The two walked across the narrow hallway and into room three. There they found a middle-aged lady lay on the stretcher, limp and sallow. Her bleached hair lay in folds across her face. Her head was turned towards her husband, whose hand she clasped limply.

"Mrs. Mickritz? This is Dr. Gary," his colleague began gently, shaking the lady, who appeared to be sleeping. Her husband scooted his chair closer to her, and touched her gently on her cheek. In truth, Gary hated to be introduced that way. Something about his mannerisms enticed all of his colleagues to introduce him as "Doctor Gary." Maybe it wasn't such a bad thing.

"Honey, the doctors are here." He spoke to her low tones, with warmth that Gary wasn't used to seeing in the ED.

The woman, a bit on the heavy side, rolled onto her back and rubbed her face. She looked uncomfortable, but not really toxic, Gary decided.

"What? When are they gonna take me to my room?" she asked, throwing one flaccid arm over her head.

The husband looked at both of them in turn. He was a ruddy-faced man with bright blue eyes, also on the corpulent side. Clearly, he was uncomfortable with the idea of taking his wife home, but whether it was because he believed her to be too severely ill, or because she had decreed that she should be admitted was unclear.

"Well, we're still trying to get your symptoms under control to see if we can treat you at home," explained Gary's colleague.

"I can't sit up, I can't eat, I can barely stay awake. I don't think I can go home." Her voice wavered as she spoke.

Her mate squeezed her hand and looked expectantly at the two.

"What we intend to do, with your doctor's advice, is to continue the fluids and the medication for nausea for the next half hour or so. If you don't feel better, we'll bring you into the hospital."

"I'm not going to feel better," she protested, rocking her head forward, weakly.

Gary decided to back off and let his colleague handle the pressured situation. He'd just met the couple, and his involvement was bound to look like the callous meddling of an outsider.

"I understand how you feel. I really think we're going in that direction. But I've seen some remarkable improvements in a short time. We haven't really had a chance for the antibiotics to work."

Watching on, Gary was tight-lipped. He was certain he'd be admitting the patient in a half-hour. The real danger was getting distracted by the other patient issues at hand, and forgetting about her. Neither he nor the nurses were likely to be unoccupied with the department, as active as it was. Making a mental note so

28

that he could re-evaluate the lady, Gary virtually leapt for the door, hoping to get out before his colleague.

"She's tough. But I don't think she's gonna turn the corner," confided Riley, as they strode together down the hall.

"No, me neither. Hell, she might even be bacteremic. She looks miserable. Have her pressures been OK?"

"Yeah, hemodynamically she's been fine. But with those shaking chills, you could be right. I just expected her to get better quicker with the IV fluids. It didn't happen. And now, my friend, I must bid you a fond adieu..."

"Got it. Thanks, man. Have a good night."

"Yeah, I will. Keep a lid on it. If either of these cases get complicated or take crazy turns that you can't deal with, call me, and I'll come back."

"You're too kind. I know you hate to sign cases out. These two are as simple as it gets. We'll get 'em taken care of. Now get out of here. You off tomorrow?"

"Yeah," said the other, triumphantly, "the whole weekend."

"What are you gonna do?"

His eyes lit up. "I have a boat down on the Cheat Lake. We're going down there early tomorrow for a couple days of water skiing with some friends from college. Should be a blast."

Gary looked at his partner, enviously.

"Well, enjoy. I'll see you next week."

Now, he thought, time to take inventory: "The kid with the wrist injury should be out of here by now; the guy with the dystonia from Phenergan just needs discharge instructions and a script; the kid with chest pain was stable and he needed to check the chest X-ray, and see if he'd gotten relief from the Toradol; the old man with vertigo would need a re-evaluation and probably admission. Add to that the lady with pyelonephritis and the other case that was signed over from Riley." Periodic recounting to himself of who was where, and what stage of care that they were in, was essential-it was tantalizingly easy to believe that a patient was on course, with all of the interventions occurring automatically after he first wrote orders, only to find that something hadn't been done, and he hadn't been notified. Failure to draw blood, or deliver a drug, or place a phone call-any of these could delay someone's care by hours. Even worse, with the distractions that beset him every few minutes, it was entirely possible to forget about a patient entirely, until someone, or something, grabbed his attention and forced him into action. Sort of like Riley's patient with the blood draw.

He frowned, as he noticed the ambulance doors slide open. That usually meant one thing.

"Doc, we tried to call but we couldn't get through-some kind of problem with our radio, I guess. Did medic command call in for us?" asked a medic with a sharp-pressed uniform, blue eyes and close-cropped hair. He frequently came to South Side and was well-regarded, both for his intelligence, his dutiful manner and his sympathy for his patients. Gary knew who he was, but failed to remember the name. He just didn't see the medics often enough to be well-acquainted with them. His partner was not someone Gary had seen before. The two were moving a stretcher bearing a very agitated woman. She was crying aloud, and speaking unintelligibly as she howled. While she repeatedly shook her head back and forth, she held a wadded towel against the left side. There was no blood on the towel. Whatever was wrong, Gary mused, she wasn't coping with it very well.

The medics rolled the wheeled stretcher into room 4, and proceeded to lift the woman off of it and onto the bed. At this point, she grabbed her left ear and let out a blood-curdling scream.

Gary looked at the familiar medic, frustrated by this unbridled display, wondering what could possibly be wrong to create such a reaction. The woman then began to heave and sob again.

The taller medic, who re-introduced himself as Pete, leaned toward Gary, in familiar fashion.

"Doc, she's got a roach in her ear. She's hysterical."

A look of resignation came over the doctor's face. So that was it. Harmless, to be sure, but truly terrible for the patient. Not a very common problem, but he'd seen it before. While someone was laying down in a bed or on the floor, a roach came scurrying across the side of the head and entered the ear. In a heartbeat, it was in too far to back out, and the patient was digging furiously at it, which probably caused the thing to crawl in even further. The last thing it would do, under attack, is try to back out. Typically, the bug went through phases of quiescence then furious spasms of activity as if trying to burrow. These little spells were very disconcerting, if not downright horrifying, to the patient.

"Ma'am," Phillips said, taking her hand in his. "I'll help you with this. I know you're upset. That thing is not going to hurt you. We'll get him out. But you have to cooperate with me."

She looked trustingly at him, blinking back the tears. But suddenly, a look of terror spread across her face and she gripped

30

him so tightly that his hand throbbed.

"It's crawling around again. It's crawling around in my ear again!"

She was a big African American lady, tall and portly, and very strong. The medics had brought her in from St. Clair Village, a housing project up in the hills behind the hospital. Again she began thrashing about, gripping her head frantically as she did so.

The emergency physician tried to hold her down, in concert with the medics, and Joann, another of the night nurses, who'd come in to help get the patient situated. Huge extremities were flying about, while the four of them were dodging and holding simultaneously. The woman was completely crazed during these intervals.

"What's her name?" Gary called out, hoping someone would answer him.

"Shequia, doc, Shequia," answered the blonde medic, trying to retain his hold on a very big thigh, as it flailed about, repeatedly lifting him off of the floor.

The physician knew he had to get control of the situation. If he couldn't talk her down, he'd have to tranquilize her with an injection-a direction he didn't want to go in for something as simple as a roach in the ear.

"Shequia," he cried out, loudly and brusquely. It was his best "I'm in control here" voice. She paused for a moment.

"Shequia," he said again, forcefully.

"You have to hold still, or I CAN'T HELP YOU!" That was plain enough, he thought. It was a bit embarrassing; he knew the entire department, and probably everyone in the waiting room, could hear his bellowing. Open confrontation was not an approach he liked to adopt.

The woman began to ease up a bit.

"Please help me," she said quietly, briefly possessed once again of her faculties.

Gary put his face very close to hers, and met her eyes with his own. He tried to appear very intense. Her dark skin and eyes made the sclera appear to shine a bright and iridescent white that shone even brighter with her tears.

"I want to help you, but you must help us. No matter what happens, I need you to remain calm. No more of this screaming. That bug in your ear may move around, but he's not going to hurt you. Here's what we're going to do. First, I put some solution in your ear, to kill him. Then, I clean out your ear. Then, you go home. But you have to work with us. Understand?"

She looked at the physician with an air of resignation.

"But," she said, pitifully. "It's a roach."

Gary nodded confidently, keeping his eyes locked on hers.

"That's actually good, honey. They're perfectly harmless. They don't sting and they don't bite. They just move around. And we're gonna stop that here shortly. Can you work with us?"

The woman finally relaxed. Joann put the head of the bed up and proceeded to get vital signs, scrawling a hasty note. Gary went to the suture cart outside the room and found a small bottle of viscous lidocaine, a local anesthetic. The gelatinous liquid would quickly suffocate the bug, and some said that the lidocaine would act as a toxin and kill it all the more dead. Either way, it was doomed.

"Now," he said gently, "turn your head and I'll put a few drops in your ear."

She did so and the liquid was instilled. Apparently, the bug objected and began to squirm again. The woman stiffened and grabbed Phillip's arm, squeezing fiercely. He looked across the room at Pete, who had been finishing up his run sheet, and who now looked bemusedly at the physician, who was quite clearly a captive in this situation. After probably a minute of this, during which his hand became waxy and white for want of blood flow, she eased her grip and sagged back into the bed. Relieved, Gary laid his hand on her shoulder. He really felt a great deal of sympathy for her, now that she wasn't screaming and disrupting the proceedings of the department.

"Better?" he asked.

She began to cry and held his hand to her face. He bowed his head as he felt the warm tears dribble down his arm. Her terror had truly exceeded all her efforts to control it.

"Oh, Holy Jesus, yes. Holy Jesus, yes," she said.

With her eyes closed, a broad, toothy smile spread across her face.

"Thank you, doctor."

"You're welcome. I'm glad I could help. Now I have to squirt some water in there and get that stuff out."

Her relief was nearly palpable.

"I don't mind, now that he's dead. Do whatever you need to do."

It was an emotional and gratifying moment. An emergency physician's days and nights were peppered with them, but there was seldom time to revel in such sequences-there was always something else to do.

32

"Now," he thought, "I have to get a hold on things." It was already shaping up to be a busy Friday night. There were charts in the box, people signing in, and he had six or seven people to take care of.

He let go of the woman's hand, noting with satisfaction that she seemed to have fallen asleep.

"Carol," he called, not really sure where she was, "can you set me up with some warm saline and a basin and syringes to irrigate an ear?"

He saw, to his frustration, that the aid was just beginning to place the splint for the young man with the wrist injury who'd he'd seen nearly an hour before. The father was sitting, patiently, watching as the plaster was molded and the ace wrap placed around it. He looked a little disgusted, and Gary hoped to avoid him. Given the size of the place, it would be very difficult. He approached slowly.

"I'm sorry this has taken so long, you should be out of here in just a couple of minutes," he said, looking at the man with an air of resignation.

Carol interjected, "I was just too busy to get over here." She clearly felt as though he was putting her on the spot and blaming her. But she was much too valuable for him to marginalize-a good aid could really make things flow. Or grind them to a halt.

"Not your fault, Carol. We just got busy so fast."

The man was more tolerant than Gary believed he would be.

"It's OK, doc. I've been watching you run around here for the last hour. You guys are trying your best. What they need around here is more help."

"You know it," Gary commiserated. "It would be great to have a second doc on until midnight or so. But a lot of nights we aren't this busy, so the hospital doesn't see the wisdom of it."

"Well, we're grateful for your care."

Gary was afraid that another delay would occur while they waited for the nurse to do the formal discharge. The skeletal crew at night meant that a lot of mundane tasks, like presenting the discharge paperwork and getting it signed, took a back seat to the bedside patient care that the nurses had to provide. He had a vision of many unhappy patients sitting in the chairs by the ambulance doors, waiting to sign the final set of papers before they could leave.

Walking briskly to the nurse's station, he pored through the charts and papers strewn there, and found the skateboarder's chart. He sat at the computer, typed in some orders and pulled them off the printer.

"Oh, I was just going to get that," Joann said, walking up behind him.

"That's OK, Jo. I really need to get some of these people moving, and you and Lizzie are busy taking off orders. I got it."

Sitting in a chair beside the injured boy, he addressed his father, reading him the discharge instructions.

"Here, sir. All I need is a signature, right here."

The man scrawled his name, patted his son on the back, and the two walked off. Gary was relieved-he had really expected the man to tear his head off.

"Hmmm...who else can I get out of here?" he wondered aloud, and pulled the charts on the boy with dystonia and the young man with chest pain.

"Lizzie-how's the guy with chest pain?" he asked over the desk, looking at her as she drew up drugs.

"He's fine, doctor. Immediate pain relief with the Toradol. What do you want to do with him?"

Gary walked over to the room, and eyeballed the man, who was sitting comfortably in the bed, talking on the portable phone.

"You OK?" he mouthed.

The man nodded vigorously, stuck his right thumb up in the air, and turned his attention back to the phone call. The EKG had not been concerning, and the chest X-ray was normal. A script for some ibuprofen, and he'd be ready to go.

He scribbled on the chart, typed up instructions for both men, and decided to check on the elderly man with vertigo. He found that the man looked somewhat better, and had now adopted a sitting position. He was talking quietly to his wife, and had a half-empty cup of ginger ale sitting beside him. Gary decided to call the PCP and recommend outpatient management and a follow up the next day, since his clinical response was so good and the studies were all normal.

Lastly, he figured he needed to admit the woman with pyelonephritis, and check the labs of the other patient who'd been signed out to him. As expected, the man's liver tests were all normal, and he quickly put the chart in the discharge rack, hoping the nurses would take care of it.

As quickly as he'd been immersed, he had been able to get the patients treated and dispositioned. He asked the secretary to place calls to the family doctor for Mr. Kitwicki. Maybe, he reasoned, it wouldn't be such a bad night after all.

Gary quickly grabbed one of the charts that that had, in the last few minutes, been placed in the rack. Staying ahead for the first few hours was imperative. After 2a.m., things often slowed to a trickle, and then he could really start to clear things out.

"Aghhh, a head lac," he announced. This usually implied, on a Friday night, that someone had been drinking and encountered some misfortune. The scalp seemed to collect a disproportionate share of such injuries. It was a dirty area to sew in, made more so by the shaving that was necessary. Too often, these wounds were from some sort of blunt trauma, and the openings were uneven, star-shaped affairs with multiple extensions and swollen, contused edges that didn't come together well. Locating the galea, the aponeurotic covering of the skull, was necessary-if it was wrenched open, it had to be repaired, to avoid a sub-galeal hematoma. Most of the time, he had to admit to himself, he couldn't find it, either because the wound wasn't deep enough, or because the irregular, macerated tissue obscured the usual planes. The threat of infection in these wounds was ever-present, and the clients were usually on the unforgiving side. It was important to be as aseptic as possible, and to irrigate effectively. Fortunately, the luxurious blood supply of the scalp mitigated the likelihood of infection, even in the really ugly wounds. But they just weren't easy wounds to deal with in a short span of time.

"Karen," he called out the door. "Could you ask someone with a free minute to bring me a liter of saline and one of those basins for irrigation?"

He realized that he had become a bit judgmental- his mind was filled with stereotypical patients that appeared to him as soon as he heard certain chief complaints in particular circumstances. Often, as he walked back through the corridor, he would wonder if the patient he envisioned would resemble the one he met when he entered the room. In this case, his suspicion that the bearer of the lacerated scalp would be a middle-aged, down-on-his-luck, inebriated man was confirmed. The patient was thin, of average height, and had long, ragged brown hair. He lay on the stretcher beside the opened suture tray, curled up on his side and shivering, as if he was cold. He held a blood-stained ice pack firmly to the side of his head with his left hand. Blood matted his hair, and had run all over the side of his face and onto his clothes, where it had clotted. The sheet on the stretcher was likewise very bloody.

One of the nurses, or perhaps Carol, had been kind enough

to open up a suture tray for him, putting out a set of size 7 sterile gloves and filling the little basins in the tray with iodine solution and saline for irrigation. The 30 or 40 ml of saline was but a drop in the bucket compared to the liter of irrigant he'd need. He'd been through this with them many times, but the message didn't seem to stick. At least, he thought, they'd tried. There was even a packet of 4-0 nylon suture on a curved needle which had been opened, his preference for minor scalp injuries.

"Sir, what happened to you?" the physician asked, announcing his presence.

The man did not stir, and Gary was briefly concerned that his head injury was the reason. He approached the bed and put his hand on the patient's shoulder. He startled awake, and turned to regard the doctor. His eyes were dull, the lids lagging. He'd been in a very deep sleep, it appeared, probably induced by with alcohol.

"Uh, Mr. Jankowski, what happened to you?" Gary reiterated.

"Oh, hiya, Doc," the man slurred. "I guess I got whacked in the head, down at Red's. You ever go down there for a shot and a beer? It's just right around the..."

"Oh, I know where it is. But, don't you know what happened to you? You know, your head injury?"

"Well, no, not really. I was drinking and carryin' on, and the next thing I knew I was on the floor. Some of my good friends over there, they got a bandage on me and helped me over to the ER. We are in the ER, aren't we?"

"Do you think someone hit you, or maybe you fell and hit your head on the way down?"

The man began to chuckle, and Gary got a full whiff of his breath, which was rather unpleasant. Moving a bit further away, the physician continued his inquiry.

"Is there anyone we can call, to figure this out? It would be good to know exactly what happened to you."

The triage sheet that the nurses had written up merely echoed what the man had said out front-he'd been drinking and suffered a head injury from uncertain source. The mechanism of injury would help to determine whether he needed a CT scan or not, to check the integrity of his skull and brain. His state of consciousness in the aftermath of the injury and his examination would play a vital role as well.

"I think you could call Red's. Ask for Schultzy. He's my good buddy. Or for Tommy. He tends bar on the weekends. Or Irene.

She's the owner. She's crazy about me."

His speech was slurred and lyrical.

Gary imagined calling the bar and speaking with his inebriated friends, if they were still there. It would probably be futile.

"Did you pass out? I mean, did you black out after your head was injured?"

"Course I did. I just woke up on the floor. They helped me up, and the next thing I know, I was over here."

"OK," the physician murmured. Although the man's memory was suspect, he'd probably lost consciousness, and that made the decision to check the head CT scan an easy one. It also brought into question the possibility of a spine fracture in the neck from his fall. The man was very drunk, and his head injury with the laceration represented a distracting injury. He would also need to have neck X-rays performed after he was placed in a stiff cervical collar and onto a backboard, to protect his neck until it was clear that things were OK. That, Gary knew, would be a challenge. He examined the man, and, aside from his laceration, could find no evidence of substantial injury, or neurologic abnormality.

"Sir, you just lay here. We'll get a CT scan to check your head and your neck, and make sure all the internal structures are OK. But I'm going to need to put a special collar on you, to protect your neck, and tape your head in place until the films are read."

The man had lost interest in the interview by this time, and had turned onto his side, curled up, and begun snoring. The small room reeked of blood and alcohol, mixed with the even more objectionable odor from the man's poor dental hygiene.

"Great," Gary muttered.

He poked his head out the doorway.

"Lizzy, this guy needs more than sutures. He probably lost consciousness, and he's too drunk for me to clear his C-spine clinically. We need him on a backboard, and I need a CT of his head."

The nurse, who had been scurrying to carry out other orders, stopped in her tracks and turned to him, a look of incredulity on her face. She had a way of squaring herself up and regarding him with a piercing glare when she was unhappy with his orders, that gave him pause.

"Doctor, do you think that for one moment he is going to stay on that board or in that collar? Forget for the moment that he can't remember what we say to him from one minute to the next.

He's really too drunk to cooperate with anyone, whether it's for his own good or not."

She was clearly exasperated. That wasn't good this early in the shift, the physician remarked to himself. He cocked his head and looked at her imploringly. He simply couldn't sit with the man and coach him for the next hour while they waited for the CT. There were too many others to see and treat. A drunken patient in the ER was a minefield: the man obviously had little regard for his health to begin with, and therefore little reason to pay any attention to what the staff said. Such a patient usually couldn't remember what he was told, anyway, and often nodded off, then awakened in a slightly less inebriated, but more unpleasant, state of mind, to find that restraining devices, IVs, tubes and collars had been placed. These served to infuriate him in his alcoholic haze. Sobriety was the only real answer, and that took time. Gary had seen various drugs administered to drunk patients to make them "cooperative," chiefly antipsychotics, but sometimes they made the behavior more bizarre or even created a greater degree of obtundation. With such altered mental status, there would be doubt about the integrity of the airway reflexes if vomiting should occur, and then it was necessary to place a breathing tube. This usually led to a whole chain of undesirable events, including admission to the ICU, more tranquilizers to keep the patient from removing the breathing tube, urinary catheters, restraints... all a very poor use of nursing, hospital and physician resources, with little to show for it when sobriety finally supervened and the patient signed out of the hospital against medical advice.

Gary stared at the man, frustrated. It was a difficult question, when one should "ramp it up" with intoxicated patients, who came with all degrees of mental status compromise. Complete coma made it simple: treat the patient as though he were critically ill. Intubation, ICU admission, IV hydration, wait for him to wake up. But, short of that, there was real risk-benefit analysis required to avoid falling down the slippery slope of over-aggressive management with diminishing returns, or even harm to the patient. One of the biggest frustrations was how a significant, or even severe, injury could be so inapparent in intoxicated patients, and then manifest itself all too well the next day, when the sensorium was no longer blunted by alcohol. All of the physicians in the group were familiar with the sinking feeling that came upon one when learning that a drunk patient, X-rayed and sutured, allowed to sober up and finally sent home from the ER, came back with something more serious that was unsuspected, in the following day or two.

Furthermore, it was widely held, but not substantiated, that such customers were contemptuous of the medical and nursing staff, and would like nothing more than a reason to bring a fat lawsuit against them. If alcohol were abolished, Gary reasoned, it would make his practice so much more pleasant.

Lizzy had already ducked into the room and placed the collar on the man, and was now assisting Carol to get him on the back board. It was a struggle, and the man was little help. He was accepting, though, for which Gary was grateful. Some drunks were fairly amiable before the sobriety robbed them of their euphoria. "We'll see how long this lasts," he mused.

"We'll see how long this lasts," Lizzy said loudly as she shuffled out of the room, heading back to the papers that she'd had to lay aside when she was interrupted.

Working quickly, Gary filled out some discharge papers and laid them in a stack next to the computers. The man with the scalp laceration had meanwhile been sent to radiology, and had returned, snoring loudly, but still able to awaken to various stimuli. The physician called up the CT scan on the computer and went over it quickly. To his eye, there were no fractures or brain injury; and no apparent bleeds. He'd wait for the call from the radiologist on the spine scan, for which he had less experience in interpretation. Meanwhile, he could begin to sew up the wound, while keeping the man on the backboard and in his cervical spine collar.

He'd been fortunate that the patient had behaved so well thus far. The physician thought perhaps he could quietly sit at the bedside, clean and numb the wound, and whip the stitches in while Mr. Jankowski was still relatively quiescent. It was an auspicious plan, though the patient had little incentive to follow through, on his end. Gary pulled up a wheeled stool, snapped on his gloves and gently irrigated the wound. Blood, hair and pieces of scalp came out at first, and then the saline ran clear. Next, he inserted his tiny 30 gauge needle beneath the skin edges in the middle of the wound, and tried to inject the lidocaine. This was clearly painful, and the man began to thrash about, grumbling and swearing.

"I'll try the rational approach, first," the physician thought.

"Sir, you have to hold still. I'm trying to make you look beautiful, again. This wound won't heal itself, you know."

The man stopped trying to toss his head about on the backboard. He seemed to process what the physician had told him, and was making an effort to cooperate. "If he can only hold still for a few more minutes," Gary thought. At least the radiologist had called with a negative report on the CT scan of the neck. Taking him off of the backboard and out of the cervical collar were keys to getting any cooperation, and, with Carol's help this was quickly accomplished. The man, now more comfortable, rapidly dozed off.

Next, he explored the injury. The wound edges were mal-aligned, swollen, and uneven. He carefully took his iris scissor and began trimming the edges, aware that each time he brought the blades of the scissors together, slicing a ribbon of flesh off the margin of the wound, the man might sense it and startle awake. For these precious few moments, he held still, but for his deep breathing and snoring. Gary could feel the deep vibration of his palate as he snored, coursing through his body and shaking the bed. He was thankful he'd never had to sleep next to anyone with such power. He tested the new margins of the wound, applying a bit of tension to the opposed edges to see if they would come together with some semblance of a neat closure. It was only a scalp, after all, he reminded himself. An ugly scar would be covered by the hair. Still, he wanted to do the best job he could, avoiding dog ears and unnecessary tension on the wound.

Suddenly, the man started, nearly sitting up on the bed. The wound drape flew off, the little bowl of iodine tipped over, and the yellow solution flew over the field, the man's hair, and Gary's lap.

"Man, I don't have time for this," the impatient physician muttered under his breath. Now, he figured, was the time to be firm.

"Look, sir. You've gotta stay still. Do you understand? I can't sew you up with you moving around like that. You have to hold still."

He raised his voice, threateningly, "DO YOU UNDERSTAND?"

The man ignored him, settled back into a comfortable position, and once again began to snore.

Gary was unhappy with the wound. He dabbed at it gently, but with enough pressure to staunch the bleeding that kept reasserting itself at the wound edges. It was an ugly, contused laceration. Despite his best efforts, the edges remained swollen and ill-defined. He'd carefully debrided the edges, removing devitalized tissue. But it still wasn't neat. Nor was it coming together as quickly as he would have liked. To his chagrin, the patient awakened again.

40

"How you doing up there, doc?" asked the man, impatiently, his speech thick and muffled by the sterile drape over his face. "I got places to go."

Gary arched his eyebrows. Where in the world would this man have to go except to bed? He wasn't fit to walk at this stage, let alone continue his merrymaking.

As an emergency physician, he knew he'd always have to work night shifts. It was part of the job. But he didn't enjoy it; the nights were just something to get through. He had never been able to "convert" to a night person. When he was working his string of overnights, he always hoped for a few minutes of peace to go to the call room and lay down. Just a bit of rest could make the night quite bearable. But in recent months, this had become progressively more rare. The ED census wasn't really up much overall, but night visits were. Unfortunately, sleeping at home, in the daylight, had become more difficult for Gary, especially with an active family. Napping wasn't really his style. So he made his way, grumbling and discontented, through his block of night shifts each month when they came up. The nights, more than any other aspect of his stressful occupation, made him look to the future, yearning for the day he could retire.

Tall and lean, Gary strode confidently through the ED, at least at the beginning of the evening. Time would take its toll, he knew, and he'd be less energetic as the night wore on. Lately, he admitted to himself, he felt his age creeping up on him. At 48, he still possessed much of his youthful energy, but every stress that he put himself through required more time from which to recover: jogging, playing football with his sons, the night shift. When he looked in the mirror, an older man looked back at him, with graying temples, crows feet, the knitted brow that never quite smoothed out. In a sense he was proud of these marks of battle-hardening, of experience, of wisdom. Thousands of hours of toil under the extreme conditions of the ED, thousands of patients presenting with myriad diseases, with thousands of different forms of suffering: treated, ameliorated, sometimes cured, sometimes not-all had left their marks upon him. Despite the stress, there was much to be proud of.

"I don't think you'll be ready to go anywhere for a while, Mr. Jankowski," he said to the man, with mock formality. "Now please hold still. How can I sew up your head if you keep moving?"

The sterile field was in near-constant motion, and he was getting irritated. But getting angry at drunken patients never seemed to help, it just made them more combative. And

41

sometimes downright unmanageable. So he tried to coax the man into more placid behavior. The alternative was to wait until the end of the shift, and then sew up the wound after the fellow had slept for a few hours. He thought about that breath, even more potent in the early morning as the blood caked in the pharynx, bacteria proliferated on the diseased gums and mucus inspissated in that dry mouth. Gary didn't relish the prospect.

He struggled with the last two sutures, drawing the wound together. The patient uttered a deep, gutteral growl with each pass of the needle through the wound margins. His breath wafted out from under the drape like a noxious cloud, and Gary could now recognize cigarette smoke mixed with the other scents.

"I could have done a better job with the local anesthetic, I guess," the physician conceded. Performing field blocks at the margins of a wound was an imperfect pursuit, sometimes working well, sometimes missing the mark widely. It seemed that some people were just resistant to the local anesthetic, and either took longer to get numb, or required more drug, or simply refused to become insensate. There was a limit, however, to time and patience and needle sticks, and sometimes you just had to sew the wound up, even if there were a few howls of protest, he noted to himself.

Gary looked over his work with some satisfaction. The ugly, contused skin edges had been drawn together with at least a semblance of their prior orientation. It didn't look too bad, particularly given the initial appearance. "Who would notice?" the physician asked himself. This man probably didn't exert a lot of energy on his vanity- a scar was just a scar, particularly above the hairline. He squirted antibacterial ointment on the wound, and nodded with satisfaction. It wasn't difficult, he mused, sewing wounds. In fact, with the glaring exception of screaming, thrashing children, it was a lot of fun. A wound, a suture tray with a packet of nylon on a cutting needle, and a few minutes of precious, uninterrupted time- that was all he needed. But the missing element, usually, was time. It was difficult to hurry the process: wound prep, local anesthetic injection, irrigation, draping, gloving, and finally closure of the wound. It simply could not be compacted into a minute or two. It was a challenge, a bit of a science project, to bring the wound back to as near an anatomic approximation as possible. When the edges came together, laced by stitches, it took on the appearance of a baseball seam or a tailor's hem: a neat, reliable, strong closure. It afforded maximum potential for healing with minimal scarring. Sometimes, the

42

deeper wounds required a layer of deep sutures as well, to eliminate any dead space where a seroma or hematoma could accumulate, inviting bacteria to set up a wound infection. Sometimes, he wished that the nurse practitioner was not finished at 10 o'clock, so that she would be able to sew up some of the late-hour lacerations, as well as seeing some of the minor "lump and bump" cases. It simply wasn't cost effective, though, to pay two providers deep into the night.

"Now listen, Mr. Jankowski, I want you to keep this wound clean and dry. Watch for infection and apply some antibacterial ointment each day after you wash it. Go to your doctor in five days to get the sutures out."

The man sat up and looked blankly at him. Turning his head from side to side, he suddenly grinned.

"I thought *you* were my doctor..."

"Well, yes. Tonight I am. But I mean your regular doctor-don't you have a doctor to look after you for your other health problems?"

The man belched loudly. "What health problems?"

He then slid backwards on the cart, dozing off once again. Gary snapped his bloody gloves into a red trash bag. These kinds of conversations could be very exasperating. He looked at the man, who now showed no evidence that he had heard what the physician had to say. "Perhaps he doesn't care," the physician thought. But he decided to provide some much-needed counseling anyway.

"Well, I'd say you drink too much. You smoke, and your blood pressure is on the high side. You're on the down side of 40 and someone should be watching your health."

Mr. Jankowski did not stir.

"Another in the endless series of patients who care not a whit for their own health," Gary fumed. On weekend nights, they made up most of his clientele. The man had had once again begun to snore loudly.

"...and I want you to quit smoking," he continued, loudly.

He knew his plea would fall on deaf, or at least indifferent, ears. Directions to put down the cigarettes seldom met with any success or acceptance in the ED population. Despite his occasional lapse when he was at work, Gary found the habit distasteful. It had touched his own family deeply-his father had died from lung cancer, and his mother, who had quit previously, had gone back to smoking after his death. Gary understood the powerful addiction potential of nicotine-one of the few drugs of abuse that he'd learned about in medical school which was capable of producing both physical and psychological addiction. It made him feel sorry for people who were caught up in its sticky web. They seldom knew what they were getting involved with until it was far too late to turn back. And there was no good way to simple enjoyment from becoming profound addiction. To be sure, only about a third of smokers died early due to the ravages of tobacco use, but that was still an awful lot of people.

He penned a few discharge instructions on the front of the chart, which were largely illegible, figuring that Maryann would somehow decipher them.

Maryann was a veteran nurse in the emergency department, having logged over twenty years there. Before that, she'd been a medical-surgical floor nurse, and had spent time in the hospital's clinic, when it had still been open. But unlike the crusty, indifferent persona that the ED brought out in so many experienced nurses, she had remained polite, caring and respectful. She was a diminutive and delightful person, and Gary loved working with her. He found her pleasant and efficient, and every time they worked together he was grateful for her competence and demeanor. Maryann's countenance had remained youthful, but she displayed an undeniable wisdom. The style of her glasses and her hair made it clear that she was no longer young, but Gary imagined that she'd looked just that way for a long time. She seemed ageless and timeless. Her dedication and devotion to nursing and her patients was obvious, but she could grouse good-naturedly about poorly administered programs and recount humorously the odd situations that arose so often in the ED. Her laugh was warm and inviting, and she was very reassuring at the bedside when patients needed that.

Occasionally, when he was traversing the corridor or sitting at the charting station, catching up on some task or other, he would observe her, or one of the other ED nurses, showing some gesture of kindness or caring. "God, what nurses can do," he would think. With all of the regulation, red-tape, documentation, computerization, standardization-nurses still found time to care for people. To explain, to soothe, to touch, to laugh. It was a beautiful thing, and he took note of it only infrequently, but it gave him a large measure of satisfaction.

He looked up at the chart rack, and glowered at the charts there. They were lined up like angry blue soldiers, challenging him, mocking him. Only an hour into the shift, and it felt as though it had already been a busy night- he'd been rushing from patient to patient without a letup. Now there were three more to be seen, and Lizzie was getting another one signed in and triaged in room two. The weariness of the night shift had begun to settle over him. The first of the charts, which he looked over as he picked it up, was that of a young woman with abdominal pain and vaginal discharge. The nursing note described that she'd had abdominal pain for a few weeks, with increasing severity of late and the development of a thick, white discharge. The dull pain was not related to eating or urination.

Striding down the hall toward the Gyn room, Gary took measure of his surroundings. The place was truly depressing. Gray walls, off-white floors, dirty drop ceilings, and chartreuse cabinets. The color scheme was ghastly. Fluorescent lights cast their unsympathetic, other-worldly glare over the corridors and inside the tight, unpleasant rooms. In the middle of the department, the work station was cluttered with dingy-looking computer consoles and scraps of paper. South Side's was a typical ER, not a bit of cheer about the place. Torn, dirty posters clung to the bulletin boards, half-hearted attempts at education of a public that so often paid no heed.

There was a rack with a slew of different patient education leaflets which the nurses or doctors would send home with those who were discharged: fever, diarrhea, nausea, dehydration, abdominal pain, constipation, headache, sprains, sore throat, sexually transmitted diseases. How often, he wondered, did patients actually pay any attention to them? How often did they get tossed into the "round file" in the parking lot before they even got to their cars? It did seem hopeless, at times. Shining a beacon of medical education from atop the emergency room in an effort to improve public health, while a noble concept, seemed to actually do very little.

And people signed in for the most trivial things, at the oddest hours. This was one of Gary's true peeves. Of course, all of them had to be seen by a doctor, even for the sniffles, in accord with the various governing bodies that administered the hospital. "Whose emergency is it, anyway?" his chairman had pounded into his head when he was in residency. "The patient's, of course, and he defines it." He'd seen enough odd complaints to answer that question with alacrity.

He paused in front of the desk, and peered over it at the mess on the other side. Karen, in her customary seat, was shuffling through several charts to take off orders. His own space was piled with papers that he had to attend to. There simply was no time, but as the night wore on, he'd probably get to them, he figured.

He thought about the numerous EDs he'd worked in when he was in training, and after he'd graduated from residency. The configurations might have been different, and the size of the rooms, but they all tended to look the same. You could quickly recognize what area of the hospital you were in. There were almost never any windows, as though any sense of the outside world was forbidden during these proceedings. Doubtless, privacy was important, but Gary surmised that windows need not be in the patient rooms. And privacy windows were always possible. Hospitals seemed to strive to separate themselves from life outside on the street, creating the sense that what happened inside of them was not a part of real life, was somehow an exception. When you worked in the ED, Gary thought, you realized just how often "real life" was interrupted by the need for health care. People always seemed so surprised to be in the emergency room.

The physician stretched and yawned, then moved his lanky frame down to room 7. Opening the door, he addressed the woman inside. She looked remarkably young, he thought. At 17, she had already twice been treated for pelvic inflammatory disease, according to the nursing history on the chart. That wasn't a rare situation, not among the youth that presented to the ED. It was perhaps unfair to classify them as some sort of demographic group, but he had the strong sense that "average" young people stayed out of the ER. Doubtless, bad luck could hit anyone, and most everyone he knew had been in the ER once or twice during their lives. But a select group of people bounced in and out with injuries and illnesses and social situations, over and over again. It had once surprised him, as it seemed so preventable, with a bit of attention to health and some reasonable standards of behavior. On the other hand, he admitted, without this reckless group, he'd have a lot less to do.

He introduced himself.

"Hello, I'm Doctor Phillips. What seems to be the problem tonight?"

She lay on the bed in a pair of pink sweatpants and a meager top that revealed her midriff. Indicating her abdominal pain, she gestured toward her jeweled, studded navel.

"It's been hurting down here- you know, like a dull pain."

"What makes it better? Or worse? What's it feel like?" he persisted, wanting more information.

46

"Well, if I lay real still, it's not too bad. But moving around hurts, and coughing hurts. It's just a pain."

"Burning? Sharp? Aching?"

She looked confused, and furrowed her brow.

"I don't know. It just hurts."

"Does it hurt when you pass your urine? Have you had any change in bowel habits?"

Gary could tell she was getting irritated with the questions, but emergency medicine was detective work, and the history and physical was supposed to be 90% of the necessary information. Furthermore, without a good H and P, it was hard to select the appropriate lab tests. It had been well demonstrated that "shotgunning" with a ton of blood tests is seldom the best way to arrive at a diagnosis. He looked sympathetically at her, and sat down on the stool in the room.

"Sorry to ask so many questions, when you don't feel good. But without talking to you like this, I have a hard time figuring out what's wrong."

She had a difficult time making eye contact, like a lot of adolescents. Shrugging in an indifferent way, she acknowledged his statement.

"That's OK."

"Let's take a look at you."

He briefly examined her eyes and throat. There was a red flush to the mucus membranes of her throat that was very familiar. Everyone who smoked had the same irritated membranes. And the corrosive smell of the smoke was impossible to miss. But there was no exudate or pus to suggest gonorrhea. The neck and chest exam were unremarkable.

He moved to the abdomen. As he palpated the soft flesh deeply, she shifted and moaned with discomfort, particularly as his hand moved toward the lower quadrants and suprapubic region. Her belly was soft, but she was quite tender. There was no evidence that the peritoneum, the lining of the abdominal cavity, was inflamed. Such a finding would imply something urgent, perhaps an inflammatory state that required surgery, such as appendicitis or ruptured diverticulitis.

As he went through the examination, Gary heard another chart drop into the rack with the characteristic thud. The sound unnerved him. Working alone at night could be intensely stressful. It ate him up inside. He felt fatigued for most of the night, and, in the wee hours, had a hard time caring about people's problems. And God help him if anyone really sick came

47

in-the whole place came to a grinding halt. One doctor and two nurses could easily be completely consumed by one seriously ill or injured patient.

His pessimism didn't reflect a lack of caring about people's welfare, or that he did not want to help them or assuage their suffering. His motivation in medicine, although somewhat jaded by experience, age and fatigue, had not really been seriously eroded. But the time spent in the ED was crazy: humping all night long to keep up with the administrative and clinical burden of caring for patients was profoundly exhausting. At quiet times, he found himself fantasizing about working eight-to-four in an orderly, quiet office, perhaps in the department of Public Health, or in industrial medicine. He saw himself calmly greeting patients, remembering them fondly from prior visits, going to lunch at a sunny sidewalk café just around the corner, returning to a waiting room full of patient people... it was a delightful vision. "Someday," he mused, "someday..."

It was strange, he recalled, that he'd ended up in emergency medicine at all. Family practice had originally been his destination. Well-baby checks, caring for the elderly, a nice mix of children, internal medicine, ob/gyn, geriatrics. Somehow, though, he'd gotten off track-the excitement of the ED had seduced him: trauma care, airway management, resuscitation of the critically ill, diagnosing and treating heart attacks-it had all seemed so vital, so important. But countless exposures to unstable patients, endless pressures to "improve quality," frustrating manipulations by people seeking opioids, and the rotating schedule- all had combined to dull the allure of the profession. It was clearly too early to retire, and Gary still felt strong and vigorous. But at times, the grind became a little too much. He was beset by such thoughts on the night shift.

The young lady cleared her throat, and the physician was transported back to the moment. He turned his attention to the case at hand.

"Maybe it's a urinary tract infection," he thought, eyeing the jeweled stud in her navel, and remembering that she had one in her tongue. He wondered why young people felt the need to get so many parts pierced and decorated with tattoos.

"I'm not sure yet," he announced to her, "but it sounds like you could have a pelvic infection again. You've got the discharge, and the tenderness in the right place, and it's similar to the symptoms you had before. Do you understand how damaging these infections are? It's really important that you practice safe

48

sex, you know, with a barrier type of contraceptive, or this could happen over and over."

She looked at him blankly. Surely, he thought, she'd heard of 'safe sex.' Weren't the schools supposed to have classes on this stuff?

"Condoms," he explained. "Does your partner use condoms?"

She showed no surprise at his candor, and readily answered.

"Mostly, yeah. But sometimes, you're in a hurry, you know, and one thing leads to another..." she smiled rather proudly, he noticed, as though her physical interactions with her partner elevated her to a higher status than one might otherwise expect of a 17 year old girl.

"Is he your only partner? It's important that he be treated too, if this is a pelvic infection. Otherwise, he could give it right back to you. You know, men get these things too, they just show it in a different way."

At this she looked unsettled, and shifted uneasily on the cot.

"He says it's my responsibility to get this taken care of. Can you just give me a prescription for him too?"

Gary shook his head.

"No, that wouldn't be appropriate. I'd have to evaluate him and make sure that we're treating the right thing. But if he signs in, we'd be happy to check him out and get him treated, too."

She was an attractive young woman, with dark, flowing hair to her shoulders and dark eyes as well. She did not seem particularly distressed to be in the ED for what was probably a sexually-transmitted disease, which bothered the emergency physician. A few more episodes like this and she'd be a real risk for ectopic pregnancies, infertility and chronic pelvic pain. It was difficult to get through to people her age about abstinence-they did what felt good to them. Not a lot different than his own generation, back in the seventies, he observed. But somehow, the behavior bothered him now, as it never would have then, certainly not when HE was involved. The morality of premarital sex didn't really disturb him, but rather the incredible lack of responsibility that these kids showed.

"OK," he said, walking towards the door. "Let's collect a urine specimen, and send some bloodwork. Also, let's do a pelvic exam, and send some cultures of your discharge."

She lay back on the table. "OK, you're the doctor."

"Right," he said, over his shoulder, as he hurried out, writing the orders for the testing as he headed for the chart rack.

"Here, Karen," he said.

The secretary looked surprisingly chipper. Gary wondered how anyone could work steady night shift. Especially in the emergency department, with all of its surprises and uncertainties. But she did it, time and again, five nights a week. Nothing seemed to faze her. No matter how many orders he wrote, no matter how many charts he laid in front of her, she pushed through the workload, entertaining the rest of them with her sarcastic humor. She had one speed only. But she got the job done, and she was always standing in the morning. She just had to be a purebred Southsider, Gary figured. He wasn't sure, but he'd have been willing to bet that Karen had been born and raised there, probably by a father who had spent his life in the steel mills. She had the distinctive Southside accent and diction to accompany her gritty determination. Fair and very overweight with a round face and short, silver-gray hair, she had a pleasant countenance, which quickly assumed a look of determination when she was under pressure. Like so many older women of central European heritage, she had severe degenerative joint disease, and she waddled more than walked. But her appearance belied her capabilities.

"Doctor," Maryann called from the charting station, concern in her voice, "it looks like a car's dropping someone off in the driveway."

She was peering out the ambulance doors.

"Uh-oh, they're taking off. And this guy they left on the sidewalk can't get up. We'd better go get him. Karen, call security..."

"I did, they're headed out right now."

Karen had a way of anticipating orders that made her a bit of a legend among the physicians. She always seemed to do the right thing, never overstepping boundaries. In almost supernatural ways, she anticipated orders and started enacting them just as they were barked out in emergent situations.

Upon hearing Maryann's description of what was happening in the driveway just outside, Gary shook his head from side to side, slowly. Most drop-offs were drug-related hits of one sort or another. The delivery service didn't care if the victim went to a trauma center or just the local ER. There was some sort of code out there on the streets: get him to the hospital, then get the hell out of there. He hoped it was just a victim of a fight or some other relatively minor trauma. If this was a gunshot wound, he figured, his night was about to get much worse.

That appeared to be exactly what it was. As he recorded his findings on the girl he'd just seen, he was able to watch the outside proceedings on one of the little black and white TV monitors that the security police sometimes scanned. He could see Maryann and the night guard placing the man on a stretcher. A pool of blood was left behind on the cement where he'd been lying. It appeared that he'd been shot through the thigh.

He sprang into action at that moment, shoving the chart with its orders across the counter to Karen, then moving quickly to the "major" room,   room1, where their infrequent trauma victims were taken. He met them as they wheeled quickly in through the ambulance door.

"Get me two IVs, Maryann. Let's get the clothes off and look him over. Looks like chest, belly and head are all OK." Gary eyeballed the victim warily, walking rapidly to the stretcher as they careened through the ambulance doors. The man was conscious.

"Sir, can you talk to me? Who did this? How many shots were fired? Where were you hit?"

The guy might not even know himself, Gary admitted, but it was worth asking. His own focus on the obvious might lead him to miss something important.

The patient, a young African American male who was well-built and handsome, swore and writhed in pain. Like many young gunshot victims, he presented angry and violent, not yet free of the adrenaline that had begun coursing through his vessels. Or perhaps the substances that caused the violence in the first place.

"Goddammit, help me! How the hell should I know who did it?"

It was a pretty standard answer. The victims of this kind of violence never seemed to know who simply drove by and riddled them with bullets.

The physician needed to know the integrity of the man's most important functions-breathing, oxygen levels, blood pressure, pulse.

"Do you have vitals, Maryann?"

She was hurriedly inflating and slowly deflating the blood pressure cuff, listening as best she could over his arm, amidst the turmoil. "His pressure is OK yet, 140 over 70. The heart rate is 110, but I guess mine would be up, too, under these circumstances."

She briefly turned to the physician and added, "His respiratory rate is 16, and the oxygen saturation is 100%."

51

She began connecting the man to the monitors and started to remove his clothing. He was very confident in Maryann. She easily could ramp it up, collecting data, starting IVs, apprising him of the situation...but she never failed to be a nurse. In the midst of human catastrophe, in which she had duties that really did comprise saving a life, she remained approachable, composed, even humorous at times. For him, it de-constructed the almost unreal atmosphere that could pervade these resuscitations-her composure lent itself to him, his thoughts were more ordered, he remained more in touch with the situation, his staff and the patient. Trauma management could be intimidating, especially if you didn't do it all the time. It was one thing to be part of a dedicated trauma team, as at the university, backed up by a round-the-clock OR team that could field virtually anything, and world-class intensive care units to care for the patient in the aftermath. But here, on the outskirts of modern medicine, it was downright scary. The resources required were often overwhelming, and none of the support personnel were particularly skilled in this area. Couple that with the potential for rapid demise in a young, previously healthy, patient, and it was a disease process that Gary hoped would pass him by.

These resuscitations could be carried out in a robot-like fashion, scripted and tightly coordinated, by a roomful of programmed automatons deftly moving through the process. Doubtless that was what would produce the best and most reliable results. But, in his environment, Gary preferred Maryann's version. When there was a spare moment, she would comfort the patient, hold his hand, ask him about his family and his home. It was basic, unexpected and marvelously caring.

The man was restless, turning this way and that. This concerned Gary, and he wondered if the internal hemorrhage was more significant than was reflected in the vital signs the nurse had reported.

The patient craned his neck to lift his head off of the table, and looked down at his leg. "Am I gonna die?" he asked quietly.

"No, I don't think this is a life-threatening injury." The physician tried to sound confident. "But it's important for you to talk to the police and let them know what happened. Anything you remember can help. We don't want to see any more people cut down like you were."

The patient looked blankly at the ceiling.

"OK, Maryann, good. Airway, breathing, cardiovascular, disability." He recalled by rote the algorithm from his trauma life support training. "Let's get all these clothes off. It looks like the bleeding has stopped, at least on the outside. His chest is clear, and his belly is soft. Help me logroll him, would you?"

She got on the opposite side, and they rolled the man toward her. The bleeding from the buttocks wound had ceased. It was a tiny, perfectly round entry wound that had clotted off nicely. A gelatinous streak of blood peeled off onto the sheet as they turned him. It was alarming and intriguing, how such a small, clean entrance wound could lead to such unbridled destruction inside the body. Once a bullet entered the body, it tumbled about with extraordinary energy, macerating tissues, fracturing bone, sending destructive shock waves radiating in all directions, with the capacity to destroy nerves and render blood vessels nonfunctional. Gary palpated the man's back, finding nothing remarkable. The genitals were normal, with no evidence of a subcutaneous bullet anywhere in the groin area. Both legs appeared normal except for a bullet entry hole on the anterior aspect of the right thigh. It was odd. Shot from behind and from the front. Maybe, he reasoned, there were two assailants, or maybe he'd spun around after the first shot, only to be hit by a second one.

"Tell Karen we need a portable chest, a KUB and a pelvis," he called to no one in particular. The chest X-ray might have been a stretch, but bullets could tumble for a quite a ways, and this was one place that he had to rule out its presence. Besides, the man would almost assuredly end up in the OR across the river at the University after stabilization, and they'd want a chest film.

Gary was thankful that his little ED didn't see too much of the "knife and gun club" action. But they saw enough, just enough, to bring care in the rest of the ED to a grinding halt. He remembered the trauma resuscitations at the University, where he'd trained. There were at least 10 people around the bed, even before the patient arrived, including nurses, therapists, medical students, surgical residents, emergency physicians and anesthesia personnel. The experienced people talked, joked, greeted each other, remarked on the lateness of the hour or the business of the season, while the young ones paced nervously, checked and re-checked their equipment, reciting their expected interventions in their minds. Still, the pleasantries ceased and the intensity rapidly came up as the medics brought the patient in. The crowd descended on the unfortunate victim with extraordinary energy, checking the vitals, firing out questions and ensuring that the rule of initial trauma resuscitation was effectively enacted: "fingers

53

and tubes in every orifice." Within a couple of minutes, IV's were placed, labs drawn and sent, the airway managed, bleeding staunched, interview and exam conducted, and therapy initiated. It was all so smoothly orchestrated. The support was incredible: in moments, there was a blood gas, hemoglobin level, electrolytes, X-rays, toxicology screen. Type 'O' blood was pre-arranged in "trauma packs," that could be grabbed and infused within a few minutes. Even CT scans were available with no waiting, around the clock. Surgical specialists of all kinds were a floor or two away. The organization of trauma care along these lines made sense; small hospitals simply couldn't offer these services. The tertiary centers saved these people's lives, if it was at all possible. But the burden of initial assessment, stabilization, referral and packaging for transport that fell on the lonely ER doc in the quiet outpost was a heavy one.

"That's what we need," he said aloud, suddenly, thinking of the extraordinary efficiency of those trauma teams.

"What's that doctor?" Maryann had overheard his mumbling. They had worked together for years, and she would never imagine calling him by his first name, or eschewing his title. Not even in a private conversation, with no one else in earshot. Lizzie was the same. It came with the territory; older nurses had been trained to keep physicians at the top of an almost mythological hierarchy. A younger nurse, after familiarity had been established, might revert to a first name basis, in a friendly conversation.

"I was just thinking about the trauma teams at the University hospital-they work so well," he confided.

"It's too bad, doctor, but here, it's just you and me. We can always call Eddie down if we need to."

She said all of this cheerfully, optimistically, recognizing that it could not be otherwise, and it would not be useful to go on about it. It gave the anxious physician little comfort that he could call down the respiratory therapist, who probably was busily engaged in delivering nebulized drugs and adjusting ventilators in the ICU.

A couple of tipsy adolescents, strolling through the ED on the way to visit a friend in one of the back rooms had stopped to watch. They were entranced; doubtless it seemed a lot like one of the medical dramas on TV, only without the good-looking cast.

"Please folks, no spectators!" Maryann called out, and they shuffled on, whispering to each other.

"Jesus, don't people have any respect?" Gary grumbled.

"No. Not when they've been drinking, doctor," the nurse observed, shaking her head.

"This is a funny place to work, sometimes, isn't it?" she asked, cocking her head and peering at him through her horned-rim glasses. For a moment, she reminded Gary of his hawkish little grandmother, his father's mother, long since deceased. She had worn a similar style of glasses through which she used to look at him with piercing blue eyes when she was telling him something important, or when he tried her patience.

"I mean, we see it all, don't we?"

"Maryann," he began, turning to her. "There is no better place to witness the entire human experience than the emergency room." He said this with a hint of pride in his voice.

He silently gave thanks that the man was stable, and moved out to see more patients while the films and labs were in progress. There were four charts in the box, and he still had to do the write-up and orders for the gunshot victim. He began to let go of the churning desire to stay abreast of the patients. Why, he wondered, was it so important to him to keep the box empty? Part of it was providing a decent service- people hated to wait. The other part of it was pride. Emergency physicians frequently boasted to each other about how many patients they'd seen on a given shift, without dwelling too much on the quality of those hurried interactions. But the setting begged for efficiency, not bedside manner. He resigned himself at this point to move as fast as he could to see the patients until there weren't any more to see, and forget about staying ahead.

"It's so damn frustrating, sometimes," he thought. "Seeing patients, and caring for them isn't usually that hard. It's the records, the administration, the documentation, the orders, the delays, the tests, the pharmacy screw-ups. If I could just see people, and think about their problems, provide care and not have to constantly fill out forms, answer phones, justify tests, track down loose ends, or sit at that damn computer to type up discharge instructions-this job could be so much more enjoyable."

"But that won't ever happen," he said allowed, turning to the secretary. "I need to write all this down for you, Karen. Doesn't it seem like the most depressing things come in during the middle of the night? I mean, even worse than daylight. Maybe the darkness makes it seem worse. How do you do this night after night?"

She rolled her large, protuberant eyeballs towards him.

"Doc, somebody has got to be here. If it weren't me, it'd be somebody else. Aren't you glad it's me?"

55

He smiled, approvingly.

"Yeah, I'm really glad it's you. Here's the orders for the guy with the gunshot wound."

Turning to her, he asked the question that had been floating around the ED for the past week. "Karen, if we do fold up, where will you go?"

"Doc, I been here for 34 years. I can't imagine going anywhere else. I'm part of this place, and it's part of me. I don't think I could bear to go to another hospital. Just too many changes. I guess I could find some other work here on the Southside."

He didn't know how to respond to that. A lot of the employees at the little hospital could measure their experience and loyalty in decades. Many, perhaps most, had never worked anywhere else. In a small way, that would not gather headlines or ripple into the city with great effect, there would be economic destitution for such people. At least, as a provider, Gary had real options.

He grabbed the next chart, walking briskly back to the corresponding exam room. An unshaven, disheveled man lay on the stretcher. He appeared indifferent, not just to his surroundings, but to life in general. The room smelled of his unwashed body, and the socks upon his feet, once white, were nearly black with scum and dirt. The blue pants he wore were stiff with grime and stains of uncertain origin. Over this, one of the gray hospital gowns had been draped by the nurses. Gary tried not to get to close to the little pile of clothes on the end of the bed. The ED was an earthy place, and he'd once before picked up body lice from a patient. His whole house had erupted over that one. Nothing wrong, he assured himself, with maintaining a respectful distance, at least until he had to touch the patient.

"What can I do for you tonight, Mr. Grdzynk?" he asked, struggling with the name.

"Doc, I don't even know why they brought me here," the man slurred.

"Seems like every time I get tanked someone drags me to the ER, at one place or another." An uneasy smile crossed his face as he looked up. His gray eyes had no sign of life.

"Forty-three years old?" thought Gary. "He looks like he's seventy-three."

He noted the weariness of the man's expression, wrinkled and devoid of emotion. His hair, uncut and matted, was an odd sort of light color that wasn't really gray, nor blond nor brown, just some unhealthy hue in between all of these. He had wadded up his tattered coat and placed it under his head like a pillow, and he lay back into a position of repose after greeting the physician. If he wasn't excited about being transported to the ED, he certainly wasn't distressed by it.

"Is there anything wrong with you? I mean, are you hurt, or sick?"

The man obviously had no real health emergency to attend to. Gary tried to be concerned, but he sometimes felt ill-used by a system that utilized the emergency department as a repository for drunks found on the street. The fear of liability led everyone to insist on medical assessment, with assumption of responsibility for the person's well-being by the hospital and the emergency physician. Doubtless this made some kind of sense in the overall context of the health-care system, but there was little justification for the time and money wasted in these pursuits. Listening briefly to the man's heart and lungs, he pulled down the lower eyelids to inspect the conjunctiva, the pink membranes along the inside of the lids. They were injected, and his throat was reddened.

"Do you smoke?"

"Course, doc. I smoke and I drink cuz I enjoy it," Mr. Grdzynk answered, in a sing-song manner.

The man was a bit nonsensical, but rather pleasant, in his inebriated state. The physician wondered what he was like when he hadn't been drinking.

"By the way, could I go take a leak?"

Gary shook his head, frowning.

"I'm not sure you can even stand, let alone stroll to the bathroom. Why don't we get you a bottle?"

The patient blinked his bloodshot eyes at the doctor, attempting to focus. He exhaled and the room smelled like a tavern immediately.

"S'allright with me. Long as I get to go."

"Does your belly hurt?" Gary asked, pressing on the man's upper abdomen. It was soft, and he didn't seem to be tender. Despite the large amount of calories the man obviously indulged in when he drank each night, he was so thin that his ribs were readily evident, as were his belly muscles. He was very poorly nourished.

"Sometimes when I drink a lot it hurts, then I drink more to kill the pain," the man explained, breaking out into peals of laughter.

His two yellow teeth protruded from his lower jaw when he

57

laughed, like a set of fangs.

At that moment, the physician was not humorously disposed. "Let's get some fluid into you. We'll check your liver and pancreas, along with your blood counts. I hate to do this, but I'm gonna have to put a finger into your rectum."

The man's eyes widened.

"What? Doc, do we hafta? There's nothing wrong back there. Let's just skip it."

Gary helped ease the patient onto his side, hiking his boxer shorts down and then lubricating his gloved finger. Despite the verbal protests, the intoxicated man was obedient, and complicit with the exam.

"Let's just get it over with. You're over 40, so you ought to have the prostate checked once in a while, anyway. We need to make sure there's no blood in the stool."

"I don't think I need this-it's pretty personal, you know," he grunted as the physician gently inserted a finger.

"It's no fun on my end, either."

Gary noted the large, soft prostate, but it had no hard or nodular portions to indicate a growth or cancer.

"No, really, pal," Gary thought, sarcastically, pulling his soiled finger out of the man's rectum, "I live for this." But it was an indispensable part of the exam. Chronic alcoholics were always anemic, and usually had some sort of abdominal discomfort, most often due to some degree of gastritis or other upper GI disorder. A rectal exam to obtain stool for blood testing was a basic part of the workup for any such person, to rule out gastrointestinal tract-related blood loss. Gary had once waited for the low hemoglobin test to come back, before suggesting the rectal exam-now, he just incorporated the digital insertion right up front. It came with the territory.

"That hurt?" he asked.

"Hell yes, it hurts. You ever have this done?"

"Yeah, once or twice. I don't like it either."

"Well, then you know what I mean. Now, I really gotta take a leak. Can you get me that jug?"

Handing the man one of the opaque plastic urine bottles, the physician frowned, wondering if he could be trusted to hit the mark.

"Here. And leave the bedrails up. Oh, for God's sake, you're gonna get urine all over the place. Do you need help?"

The man struggled to urinate, trying to place his penis, which just protruded from his pants, into the mouth of the bottle.

"Hold it. Let's get your pants off."

Gary sighed. Just then, Lizzy, energetic and all business, appeared at the doorway. Her white dress and white hose were pressed and pristine. The relaxed "blues" scrub uniforms were not for her, though many of the other nurses wore them, especially when they were on the overnight shift. Occasionally, Lizzy would wear her nursing cap, a vestige of days gone by.

"Doctor, the X-rays are back for the man in bed 2. And I'm ready for that pelvic exam when you are."

"OK, Lizzy-thanks. Can you help this gentleman hit the bottle? I've got to reexamine that fellow in two."

She narrowed her eyes, grimaced and walked into the room. Lizzy had a strong sense of propriety, having been educated in an era of greater personal responsibility. She seldom shrugged off bad behavior as a "sign of the times." Gary could tell she was about to deliver a public health message, and made himself scarce.

"You need to knock off this drinking. You're gonna kill yourself. They drag you in here like this almost every week," she spit out angrily, donning latex gloves with a snap.

"Well, I'll do my best for you, sweetie," the man retorted, and sighed as he began to fill the bottle.

Gary left the room only to find himself face-to-face with a rather short man, wearing a brown hat that reminded the physician of a nineteen-fifties detective movie. He had thick glasses that magnified his soft brown eyes, so that they floated behind the lenses as though they were suspended in two small fishbowls. He was elderly, with silver hair, and his neat, well-pressed suit smelled of mothballs. He appeared apprehensive, and his movements were very staccato, like a little bird.

The diminutive man addressed the doctor in a hesitant, pleading voice. "It's my brother, doctor. Can you check him out? I had to bring him in. He's not acting right. He has a headache, and he's restless. He won't eat anything. My mother has been taking care of him. But she's had a colostomy, and she can't keep up with him anymore."

"Does your brother get headaches a lot? Or is this something new?" the emergency physician asked, regarding this concerned little man with curiosity.

"I don't know," the man looked perplexed. "He can't really talk. He's never talked. He's kind of slow."

"When did the headache start? Was it sudden?"

They walked into the exam room adjacent to the one he'd

59

just left. There, a man sat on the stretcher, peering at them. He didn't look physically ill, but something was obviously wrong with him. He looked about in a simple-minded, accepting fashion, almost smiling, but not quite. He grunted when spoken to, but did not form words or follow commands. When he noticed his brother coming into the room, his large lips curled into a grin. They framed a very poorly-kept set of teeth, riddled with caries and set in reddened, swollen gums.

"How long did you say the headache has been there, sir?" Gary asked, repeating the question.

The man shifted unsteadily on his feet, and quickly took his hat off, as though afraid of offending the physician by wearing it indoors. "I think it started today, when he came back from the hospital."

"Hospital? What hospital?"

"He was in the psychiatric institute over at the University."

"For what? How long?" Gary was now perplexed.

"About two weeks. They just let him go today. I'm not sure what they diagnosed while he was there. He just wasn't acting right at home, so we took him to get evaluated, and they kept him."

" Mr. uh..."

"Razkosky. Joseph Razkosky. This is Bartholomew." He indicated the brother.

"Yes. Mr. Razkosky, how long since he has acted 'right?'"

The little man's eyes darted about, uneasily.

"Well, he's always been slow. He couldn't go to school. Ma kept him home and took care of him. I just don't think she can do it anymore."

"Your mother must be an amazing woman. Bartholomew can't do much on his own, can he? I mean, can he feed himself or bathe or go to the bathroom?"

"Well, doctor, no. Not very well. Not by himself. But with ma's help and mine, he does okay."

The emergency physician was beginning to see the picture. This man, with severe mental developmental issues, probably from some birth injury or a congenital problem, had been sheltered for nearly sixty years, by a protective mother and loving brother. And now, with age and their own infirmities, the pair could no longer continue to care for him. He examined the patient, observing his cranial nerve function, strength, sensation and ability to grasp and display coordination-at least, he did the best he could given the man's mental incapacity. The exam was

60

certainly, abnormal, but not for this patient. This he confirmed with the brother, who stood, looking on. The patient couldn't follow commands or answer questions, which was also his baseline. The rest of the exam was pretty unremarkable, save for poor hygiene.

Patients with mental disabilities made Gary a bit uneasy. Some of them were very permissive, not moving a muscle during the exam, just watching on in silence. Others would tolerate the physical contact to a point, then start to push his hand away, crying or braying or protesting. A few were completely intolerant form the beginning of the encounter, becoming progressively more hostile. Certainly, in this ER, they were usually full grown adults, not children, and they were often very strong. A good, supportive caretaker was essential for control.

Fortunately, Bartholomew was of a peaceful nature. He let his eyes rest gently on the physician, offering no resistance as the exam progressed, following directions as best he could. His level of functioning was very low, and he frequently looked at his brother for cues as to how to react. The ear exam was always a treat, as these patients seldom tolerated any sort of cleaning, except perhaps under anesthesia. To Gary's surprise, the man's ears were not packed with cerumen, the drums were visible and appeared normal. Advanced periodontal disease greeted him during the mouth and throat exam, but the tonsils were unimpressive. A quick percussion over the frontal and maxillary sinuses was unrewarding, and the lymph nodes of the neck were not palpably enlarged. He certainly had no trouble flexing his neck, and there was no fever. The perplexed physician doubted that the headache was anything serious. He wondered how the brother had even come to understand that Bartholomew had a headache, but after 60 years of living together, relying on mostly non-verbal communication, he assumed that they had a language all their own.

"Mr. Razkosky, when you found out about the headache, did you by any chance call the doctors who discharged him today?"

"Well, I tried. The hospital over there isn't an easy place to deal with. When I called I asked for the psychiatry doctor that he is supposed to follow up with, but they told me he's not in, and that I should call back on Monday. I didn't know what to do. I'm not sure they did anything for him, over there. I thought I better bring him here for a second opinion."

Wincing, Gary tried to avoid looking perturbed. This was a disposition problem, a request for placement, pure and simple. It

61

would be nearly impossible to get anything done to address this family's needs this night. And no primary physician would be interested in admitting the patient tonight for a social problem, when there was no apparent acute medical problem. It would be reasonable to look at some X-rays to make sure that his frontal or maxillary sinus cavities weren't occluded and opacified. But he doubted the need for a million-dollar workup, here. The man didn't look ill, the exam was benign, and the story was a bit dubious. Meanwhile, he'd have to begin to grapple with the mental health system.

"Sir, let's get our psychiatric people involved. Maybe they have something they can offer to your brother. I don't think the headache is really a big problem. His exam is pretty normal, for him. I'll try to get records from the psych hospital and figure out what they did. Did he have a CT scan over there?"

"Yes, I think he did, doctor," the little many said, officiously. "They said it was normal. Do you think you can help him? I can't take him home-I can't take care of him when he's sick like this."

A recent normal CT markedly reduced his fears of an intracranial structural process as the cause of the headache, and there had been no recent trauma or evidence of an inflammatory condition. Headache had a myriad of potential causes: most were due to stress, or some functional cause, like the vasodilatation of a migraine. A few were due to mechanical causes, such as a tumor, abscess or blockage of the fluid that bathes the brain. Then there were infectious causes, such as meningitis, brain abscess or sinusitis. Finally, brain swelling could occur for a variety of reasons. But the stress headache seemed most likely, with no change from his baseline exam, no tenderness, no signs of infection and no worsening of mental function. A couple of acetaminophen tablets, and a referral to psych ought to get things on the right track.

At least once a shift, Gary encountered a situation such as this: a purely social situation, with little or no medical overtones. It put him in mind of his years in residency, when he and the other housestaff raced to avoid involvement in such cases. In those days, Gary had had little respect for social disposition quandaries, psychiatric deteriorations, or cultural clashes as the underlying reasons for a patient showing up in the ED. These sorts of problems required little of what he had then considered "sophisticated" evaluation, judgment and management. However, these presentations were astonishingly common in typical emergency medicine practice. And, handled poorly, they became a true source of frustration, with the patient and family just waiting on the sidelines for someone to pay attention-until, diverting his attention from more acute medical matters, the doctor on duty remembered to do something for them. At the end of his shift, more than once, Gary had been faced with the startling realization that he'd failed to start the process of a psychiatric or social work evaluation- that he'd merely embarked on a "medical clearance" with an exam and some lab tests. Unfortunately, even after these had proven to be unremarkable, the rest of the pathway to admission or transfer could take hours. Not to mention the irritation and inconvenience for the patient and family, who had waited for considerable period, only to find that little had actually been done to address the dilemma that faced them.

"We'll do our best, sir. I'll get him something to eat and some Tylenol for the headache."

He sailed back into the hallway, calling to the secretary.

"Karen, can you call our friends on psychiatry and see if they can come down to see this patient? I have a feeling the earlier we get this ball rolling the better. Meantime, let's get a discharge record from over at Western Psych, if it's available, and his last set of chemistries and glucose. If that CT report is available, get that, too. And, let's feed him, while we're at it."

"Doctor," called the older of the two nurses, poking her head through the doorway. "I just stuck an older lady with chest pain into room two. She looks pretty pale-can I get the labs and EKG rolling?"

"Of course, Lizzy. And ask for a portable chest film and cardiac enzymes-you know, the usual. I'll be there in just a minute."

Nurses were forever commenting on peoples' color, he thought to himself. "Pallor" as a descriptor simply didn't help him much. Pretty much every patient who didn't feel well seemed to be pale. Changes in vasomotor tone are the usual when patients get stressed or sick. Small blood vessels in the skin constrict, shunting blood to more important places, in case it's needed. The normally ruddy complexion then becomes pale. It was something you could count on. Nurses didn't seem to learn that sort of thing, at least not in the depth that physicians did. Still, when a nurse got the sense that someone wasn't doing well, he'd learned to listen. How many times during his internship and residency, when he was on the spot to prove his competence and his confidence as a physician, had found it necessary to yield to the observations of a bedside nurse, he wondered. Their powers of observation, their

63

physical commitment to patient care simply could not be overlooked. A good clinician, who knew and trusted his nurse, put as much stock in these things as he did in his own senses.

He paused for a moment, watching the mentally impaired man's brother, who sat patiently beside Bartholomew, holding food up to his mouth, dabbing at him with a napkin, brushing crumbs off of his lap. He was fastidious, which explained why the patient did not appear disheveled or soiled. For over six decades, this man had taken care of his developmentally-delayed, shut-in brother, Gary observed. He felt a strong sense of admiration for this devoted man. There was no honor, no glory, no tangible reward-just caring and smoothing over endless bumps in the road. Taking care of someone with whom you could not communicate, who was not able to conduct basic acts of hygiene, was simply heroic. Every day, there would be a thousand obstacles or hurdles to clear. The most minor task-putting on pants, having a meal, going to the bathroom, taking a shower- was filled with difficulties, might even prove impossible. He put himself in the brother's place, could feel only frustration, endless frustration. "How does he do it?" he asked himself. With feeding complete, the guardian had stationed himself outside his brother's room, and patrolled a small segment of the hallway, wearing a grim but determined expression.

1a.m.

"Oh, yeah, the chest pain lady," the physician reminded himself, but at that moment he was distracted by the sound of angry cries from the triage area. A police cruiser had pulled up outside-doubtless some reveler had given an officer too much grief.

He ignored the commotion, assuming the police had things under control, and found his way into room one. A thin, gray-haired woman with milk-white skin that seemed nearly transluscent peered at him through thick glasses, with pearly frames.

"Hello, Ma'am, what seems to be the problem tonight? Are you still having the pain in your chest that the nurse told me about?"

"Yes, doctor. It's like a catch in my chest," she said, pointing to her left breast. "It's worse when I breathe."

"I see. Are you short of breath? Any nausea?"

She looked at him intently through her horned-rim glasses, with sparkling blue eyes that made it immediately clear that her eighty-odd years had not dulled her mental acuity in the least. Her speech was clear and her diction precise. She seemed more educated than most of the local population that came to the ED for care. The Southsiders were mostly blue-collar people who were descended from central Europeans who'd come to Pittsburgh for jobs in the once-ubiquitous steel mills, during the heyday of big steel, in the early part of the 20th century. Gary wondered if this woman had been a schoolteacher, or a nurse, perhaps. She took great care to describe her symptoms, and, even though she was uncomfortable, she was very respectful of both Gary and the nurses.

"Well, it hurts when I try to take a deep breath, but I don't really think I'm short of breath. And I haven't had any nausea." She confirmed and demonstrated her impressions by taking a series of profound breaths, her chest heaving visibly.

"Did you ever have this before? Do you have any history of heart problems, or lung disease?"

"No, sir. I have a thyroid condition, and high blood pressure. I also had my colon out for a precancerous condition five years ago, or so."

His eyes moved to the EKG hanging off the front of the chart.

"She's tachycardic," he said quietly to himself, referring to the elevated heart rate. "I wonder why?"

The EKG was not otherwise very remarkable. There was a left axis deviation, common in patients with hypertension. But there was nothing in the ST segments or the T waves to suggest poor blood flow through one of the coronary arteries- evidence of a heart attack, or an impending one.

He examined her, noting a mildly elevated blood pressure along with the rapid pulse. Her face was sallow, but there was no jaundice, nor were her conjunctiva particularly pale. Her oral mucous membranes looked normal, and her neck was slender, marked by the sagging flesh with which most older women eventually were graced. He listened carefully to the heart, which was beating quickly, but without any unusual sounds to suggest acute valvular dysfunction, or pericardial inflammation. There was little else to gain from the cardiac examination; the heart sounds often were not abnormal, even when there was pathology involving the heart. Her lungs were clear, her chest cage not tender. The abdomen was soft and doughy, and the legs possessed but a trace of edema, along with the usual spidery varicose veins that told of many years of hard work on her feet, or perhaps on

65

hands and knees. It was unfortunately common that the physical exam lent little to the differential diagnosis in patients with chest pain. The history was much more useful, in many cases.

"Let's try to get your pain controlled," he said to her. "And take a look at your heart enzymes and chest X-ray. I'll get in touch with your doctor when the lab work comes back. I'm sure we'll be keeping you in the hospital, given the nature of this pain, and your age. I'm still not exactly sure what's causing it."

She looked resigned. "OK, doctor. Whatever you can do to help me with this pain, I appreciate."

Older people hated to stay in the hospital; perhaps they counted it against the days they thought they had left. Bad company, bad food, bad roommates, bad décor. And too often, surly nursing and attendant staff. Who would want to check into that? Gary had seen innumerable battles, particularly between older men and their insistent wives, related to being admitted to the hospital. More striking was the common refusal of older, usually widowed, ladies, to stay in the hospital because their cats required care. Some bartered to return for admission after feeding the animals and arranging for them to be taken care of during their stay. It was touching to witness such devotion to their feline roommates.

He walked slowly out of the room, immersed in thought. He reviewed the differential diagnosis as he shuffled along. "Pneumonia, infarction, pericarditis, pulmonary embolus, aortic dissection, pneumothorax, esophageal spasm... What else?"

"Tachycardia," he repeated to himself. "I hate unexplained tachycardia." A rapid heart rate could mean many things: impending death, anxiety, pain, inflammation, infection, fear, embolism, myocardial ischemia. Its persistence in the face of treatment would be especially disturbing, and likely to indicate a more serious cause.

While awaiting some confirmatory lab work, he'd have to try to treat the problem. Leaving chest pain that might be due to myocardial ischemia untreated might lead to injury of the heart, or even a life-threatening complication. Half the time, clinicians misdiagnosed chest pain related to cardiac ischemia. Even many people with known angina and coronary artery disease had "silent" ischemic episodes: the heart deprived of its blood supply without really telling anyone. That, Gary had long ago concluded, was downright spooky. So much of the diagnoses in medicine were built upon the obvious: heart attacks caused chest pain, bacterial infection caused fever, broken necks caused pain on

66

movement of the spine. But it had become increasingly clear, as researchers peeled back the layers and systematically studied the presentation of various disease entities, that "textbook" presentations were not necessarily the norm, and in fact might occur only in a minority of patients. Further, virtually all disease states existed along the lines of a continuum-mild, moderate, severe, advanced. Symptoms in one of these sectors of disease progression might change substantially when the patient moved to the next, more severe level. In the emergency department, it was often impossible to know where patients were on this continuum. It was imperative to be aggressive with therapy, early in the presentation. If the diagnosis was found to lay elsewhere, withdrawing and redirecting therapy wasn't usually too difficult.

"Lizzy. Would you give our lady in room one a spray of sublingual nitroglycerine and some paste? On second thought, can you please start an infusion of nitroglycerine, after the two sprays, at ten micrograms per minute, and titrate to relief?"

Even though her overall appearance did not suggest serious illness, it was appropriate to assume the worst and treat accordingly. If her pain turned out to be benign, that was all well and good, perhaps money and time had been ill-used, but no harm was done. But to presume an innocent etiology of the pain, and treat it with an analgesic and discharge home with follow-up as an outpatient, could prove to be disastrous if the problem was more severe, such as the early stages of a heart attack, or a blood clot to the lung. These conditions could worsen quickly, even becoming life-threats in a matter of minutes.

Gary was certain that she deserved admission with the usual therapy for a potential interruption of blood flow to the heart, unless another explanation became obvious during the workup.

"Aspirin, too?" the nurse asked, heading for the medication room.

"Yes, yes, if she's not on it already."

The commotion from triage now had moved into the ED proper.

"Get this shit out of my eyes!" screamed a furious and disheveled young man as the police walked him into the department, his hands cuffed behind him. Tears were streaming down his face, and he was tossing his head from side to side. Clearly, he wanted his hands free so he could wipe his irritated eyes.

Gary eyeballed the policeman, who walked menacingly alongside the patient.

"What happened, officer?" he asked, a note of irritation in his voice. The police were forever bringing drunk, angry, frustrated fugitives into the ER after they were subdued with pepper spray. Usually, the patients had lacerations or other injuries from whatever struggle had occurred when they were arrested, and, sometimes, facial fractures. This particular angry young man was tattooed and pierced in a variety of places, and he was finding creative new ways to curse. Blood oozed from a laceration below his eye, and it mixed with tears as it ran down his face.

"Sorry, doc. He fought like crazy when we came to get him at the bar right down here on the corner. He was causing some kind of disturbance, but he got really out of hand when we showed up. Had to spray him with pepper a few times..."

Most of the police he interacted with were respectful and dutiful. But they were always in a hurry, as though the case they brought in was the only one in the ED. And they never seemed to come in during quiet moments- it was always when it was very busy.

The man howled derisively. "I'm gonna sue you, you son of a bitch. I didn't do a damn thing to deserve this. That girl wanted to be with ME. I was making sure that jerk left her alone!" He choked on an angry sob.

"You didn't have any reason to do this to me." His tone had now changed to a plea.

"Can't you just sew me up and let me go home? What the hell did I do?" The speech was thick and slurred.

"I'll be in as soon as I can," Gary told them, frowning. Sewing people up under pressure of time was bad enough. Sewing up facial lacerations in drunk, vindictive prisoners while the police watched on, urging him to get done quickly, was much worse.

"How long do you think it'll take, doc?" the taller of the two policemen asked. "We gotta get this guy to the jail and get back out. It's gonna be a rough night on Carson Street. Must be the moon-we've already been to two other ERs tonight."

Gary remembered the main drag down through the south side from his years in college: boarded up shops, depressing little taverns on every corner with glowing neon signs in small, dark windows. Drunks and derelicts ambled slowly along the broken sidewalks. The resurgence of the Southside neighborhood in the last 20 years had been remarkable, with upscale restaurants appearing, nightclubs muscling out the "mill-hunkie" taverns, and

68

the wholesale dismantling of the mills themselves. Now, you had to go looking for a steel mill to find one in Pittsburgh. Property values on the Southside, once near the bottom of the scale, had dramatically risen. The quiet, deserted streets he remembered now teemed with rollicking young revelers, particularly on weekends. They ambled aimlessly up and down Carson Street in small packs, ducking into this bar and then the next, like a parade that did not begin or end, threading its way from one end of the long boulevard to the other, and back again. Not uncommonly, they spilled into the streets and the surrounding neighborhoods, irritating the locals with late night antics and public urination. The upshot was that drunken kids filed into the ED every Friday and Saturday night, a wholly undesirable state of affairs. Some had real health issues, but unfortunately, many were brought in by police to be "cleared" for jail after a bit of physical injury from a fight or the apprehension itself.

The officer shoved the man gently toward his empty exam room.

"Don't worry, pal. Doc here is gonna get you looking good again."

At this, the policeman's partner looked toward the ceiling, suppressing the urge to laugh. On his best day, the physician thought, this pugnacious man probably doesn't look good. Still, he felt some sympathy for the man. Patients who came in escorted by the police virtually always were hostile, swearing, and drunk. As time passed, these unfortunates began to discern their true circumstances through the ebbing haze of alcohol, and the attitude often changed to one of real sorrow. Sometimes they wept, bitter tears of squandered lives. Afterwards, they would sullenly recount their circumstances from under the drape, as he sewed and murmured sympathetically to them. Sometimes such patients just stayed angry and passed out. Gary liked it when they simply mellowed and went to sleep, so that he could close their wounds without interruption. He found it difficult to simultaneously converse, concentrate on the wound, and keep his ears open for happenings outside the room, in the rest of the department.

"Just set up a suture tray, Carol," he called "and ask them to update his tetanus, if he needs it. I'll have to irrigate him, too- would you set me up a syringe and saline."

He hastened into the room behind the policeman, and conducted a rapid, if cursory, physical exam.

The patient had no patience for his requests, and continued

69

to growl and curse. Gary looked into the ears, which were filled with waxy cerumen. It was difficult to see the eardrums, to look for blood or fluid behind them that might indicate a basilar skull fracture. Trying to examine the man's cranial nerve function, he followed the motions of his facial and eye muscles.

"Can you just look at my finger?" he asked the restless man, the skin of whose face was beet red and obviously very irritated.

"I can't even see your finger-these assholes pepper-sprayed me," he snarled, curling his lips to reveal tobacco-stained, teeth, many of which had been broken or chipped. The man's features were broad and strong, but not handsome. His hands were thick, his arms sinewy and substantial. Gary wondered if he was a roofer or perhaps a stonemason.

"Watch the language, pal. Doc here, doesn't like swearing. Do you want me to hold him down, doc?" the smaller of the two policemen asked, staring at the patient suspiciously. Despite his black uniform and military bearing, he was slight and balding. He didn't look capable of subduing his prisoner.

The bigger policeman stood up, leaning forward in a way that made the emergency physician feel glad he wasn't the one under arrest. He suspected that they had roughed up the intoxicated man more than was absolutely necessary, and probably in retaliation for hitting or kicking at them in the struggle to make the arrest. It was a very rough job, he surmised, being a cop. He wondered how many prisoners he'd examined in the ED that were injured in a scuffle that really need not have happened.

"No, we'll manage, I think," he answered curtly.

"Hey doc," the larger cop suddenly said. "Word is out they're gonna close this place. That true? If it is, we'll be spending a whole lot more time at Mercy. That place drives me crazy-they keep us in there forever."

"Nobody knows," he answered, frowning. "Right now, it's just talk. They sure don't tell us anything. Someday, I might come in here to find the doors barred."

It irritated him that people on the street were gossiping about his future, and the future of the hospital. He looked at the patient, the tears mixing with the blood from his brow on his flushed, irritated face. The man presented a truly pathetic site. Changing his tone, Gary hoped that a gentle manner might bring better cooperation.

"Look, uh....Kurt," he said, eyeballing the chart to get the man's name. "I've got to examine you. Tomorrow, all of this will

70

hurt like hell. I don't know how bad it is-if you work with me, we'll get you taken care of. I know you're pissed off, but I can't help what happened. What I can do is start to treat you, and sew you up. First, I need to look you over."

"There. Look left, now right. Uh-huh." He moved his finger in a series of practiced motions in front of the patient's face, trying to elicit the appropriate responses of eye motion from the three cranial nerves on each side, which controlled the ocular muscles.

The orbit had begun to swell, and the eye was barely visible now. He called for the nursing aid to help him pry the lids apart, so he could hold a bent paper clip under the swollen eyelid, to better observe the motions that the globe made. The cornea was clear, and there was no blood in the anterior chamber of the eye.

"Can you look up?" he asked. The left eye did not move, but the uninjured one did. It was always a bit creepy for Gary, to see the eyes pointing in different direction.

"Kurt, do you have blurry vision? Or double vision?"

The man considered the question for a moment.

"Yeah. I mean, it looks double when I try to look up like that."

"It looks like you have a 'blow out fracture.' The muscle on the bottom of the eye is trapped in the broken bone fragments underneath it, in the orbit, so the eye can't look upwards. We'll need X-rays, but this looks pretty conclusive from the exam."

The man groaned, "that's just freakin' great." He apparently was mindful, even in his state of intoxication, of what the police officer had told him about profanity.

The physician finished the neurologic exam, then weighed the merits of a CT scan. If the man had had enough trauma to break his face, and he had altered mental status from the alcohol, it was prudent to obtain one. But everything else looked negative, and the incidence of intracranial injury with facial fractures was known to be low, he reasoned. Low, but appreciable. With his relatively normal neurologic exam, save for what appeared to be the results of drinking alcohol, brain injury seemed unlikely. Still, getting the scan would give him a greater sense of having "covered the bases," besides getting the angry man and the police out of the department for a few minutes, while he took care of other things. Then maybe he could sew up the facial wound in peace.

He handed an order sheet to the secretary, and hastily scrawled a note.

"Doctor, are you ready for that pelvic?" Lizzy asked, waddling slowly toward the desk where Phillips sat.

A moan from room one reminded him of the man with the gunshot wound.

"Are those his films?" he asked, pointing to a stack of jackets on the counter at the nursing station.

Karen nodded distractedly, while she picked at the computer keyboard. He picked up the jackets, and headed into the back room to look them over.

"Let's see," he thought aloud. "The chest is normal. The pelvis... aah, there's the bullet."

One of the missiles had tumbled around in the pelvis and appeared to be lying on the left side, though it had probably been the one that had entered through the right buttock. Phillips wondered what structures it had traversed in its path through the man. Colon, bladder, big veins and arteries, nerve plexuses, prostate-all were potentially in its destructive path. And there was no telling what a bullet would do once it entered the body. There were all sorts of interesting scientific terms, like "yaw" and "pitch", to describe how the projectile turned human flesh into dysfunctional, bloody pulp. He recalled videos of bullets fired into gel that showed how the devastating shock waves propagated radially from the actual path of the bullet, potentially injuring nerves, vessels, bone and viscera far from where the clinician might suspect. High energy, penetrating trauma was a trap, for physician and patient alike. Too many things could go wrong, and be relatively silent on presentation.

"Karen, I have to get him out of here. Can you get me the trauma service at the University? And Lizzie, would you get me another set of vitals and track down his labs? Where are they?"

As if the lab values really mattered, he thought. The guy almost certainly needed surgical exploration.

He walked quickly to the bedside, wondering how long it would take to arrange transport to the University Hospital, which was but a mile or so away, across the river.

"How are you Mr. Smith?" he asked the lean, tall man.

"Can you give me something else for pain?" was the only answer. The man's face was contorted with his suffering. But he was exceedingly calm, and lay quite still. Gary looked up at the monitor, wondering if this stoic African American man was going into hypovolemic shock. The vital signs were very similar to those he'd displayed on arrival. That did not mean he was not approaching a precipice, compensating valiantly for internal bleeding until the point was reached at which the heart and vessels could no longer maintain pressure, as the precious fluid leaked out into his pelvis. Fearing that such might be the case, despite the IV fluids he'd been given Gary was suddenly anxious about the outcome. The clinical course and the X-rays had changed his impression, and the man needed help urgently.

"Of course we can. One thing I need to let you know, one of those bullets went from your leg up into your pelvis. I think this could be very serious, and you may be bleeding internally."

The man looked surprised. He was suddenly energized.

"What are you talking about-I only got hit in the butt and the leg!"

"It looks like more than that. Bullets can take very strange paths. I'm going to have to send you over to the University hospital, where the trauma doctors can take care of you."

He appeared resigned, and sighed, again allowing his head to fall back on the stretcher. One more bad break, Gary figured, in a life full of bad breaks.

"Whatever you say, doc. But I need something for pain." He became silent once again.

Lizzy shuffled hurriedly hurried into the room, announcing that the patient's labs had come back.

"They all look pretty normal to me," she noted.

Gary glanced at them, and watched closely as the automatic blood pressure cuff inflated, waiting for the pressure to show up on the monitor. Unlike the prior one, taken five minutes before, it was low. At 85/50, it was significantly lower than when he'd come in. And the heart rate was still fast, too fast. Doubtless, the anxious physician surmised, the man was hemorrhaging, and would need to be in the OR soon.

Young people could be so deceptive after trauma. Penetrating trauma, in particular. Violent, sudden, internally devastating. An anxious, pain-wracked youth is brought in, but the exam is often unimpressive: a little pale and anxious, a bit tachycardic, the respiratory rate is up. But, they perfuse their organs, they make urine, they maintain their blood pressure, they stay alert. The physician initiates therapy, sends off the labs, looks over the X-rays and scans, and sets up a transfer to the trauma center. And then, with frightening suddenness, the patient can fall off the precipice-the internal bleeding, so precariously hidden, overwhelms the compensatory reflexes, and shock quickly supervenes. The downhill spiral is rapid, and, if not anticipated, potentially deadly. The presentation could be so deceptively benign. Gary had seen this precipitous death spiral in a few victims of knife wounds or gunshots: apparently stable at first, then in cardiac arrest a few minutes or a half-hour later, usually from brisk internal hemorrhage that was not detectable on the initial exam. Even though experience had taught him this, the phenomenon still impressed him.

"Well, Lizzy, let's hold on the pain meds till I can get this blood pressure back in a reasonable range. I'll let the trauma service know."

"Come on," he thought, "call me about this guy. I don't have a lot to offer at this point, if his pressure is falling even with the volume infusing."

"Doc," the secretary interrupted, "I have the trauma resident on call. Can you talk to him now?"

He walked to the nursing station, and presented the case to the waiting resident. A few questions were asked, and then the trauma doc apparently began to understand the urgent nature of the case. Preparations should be made for the transfer, he advised, and he would alert the OR at University to be ready. Meanwhile, the trauma attending would be paged and would call back momentarily, he said.

"Right," Gary retorted. "we've updated the tetanus, started two lines, given two liters of fluid and we're about to hang two units of "O" negative blood. We'll call for the ambulance now, but it may take five or ten minutes to get here. Even the city medics take a few minutes to get here and load the patient."

He hung up, looking around quickly, to see where his staff was.

"OK, Karen. I need two units of O-negative blood from the blood bank as in 'right now.' Lizzy, please hang it as soon as it gets here, and get it in fast. I want one unit in before he leaves here. And, Karen, could you call the city medics to see if they can transport? We don't have time to wait for a private service."

Satisfied for the moment with the course of events, Gary grabbed a chart and headed into a room where another patient awaited him. He was faced with a rather corpulent, middle-aged woman who appeared to be exhausted and uncomfortable. She lay on her side with a washcloth on her brow and a basin clutched in her hands. At least it wasn't full, he noted. According to the chart, she was a diabetic who had developed a urinary tract infection four days prior, which had been diagnosed over the phone, and a script for an antibiotic had been called in by her PCP. After two days on antibiotics, she had developed fever and abdominal discomfort in both lower quadrants. Vomiting and headache ensued, and she'd finally made her way to the emergency room.

74

Introducing himself, he began the interview, quickly ascertaining that she had a normal mental status. She knew who she was and where she was, and answered questions appropriately. Important factors in the exam of a patient with headache and fever, as delirium could signal septicemia- bacteria coursing through the bloodstream, leaving destruction and organ dysfunction in their wake- or, even worse, meningitis.

"This headache is killing me," she complained, not bothering to take the washcloth off of her face.

"Are you nauseated now?" The emergency physician was sympathetic. She really looked miserable.

"Yes," she replied. "and it hurts down here." She pointed to both lower quadrants of her abdomen.

"How about your back, in the flanks?" he asked, pointing to his low back on both sides. Clearly, she couldn't see his gesture, and he immediately wondered why he'd made it.

"A little achy, I guess."

He continued, though she was obviously not in the mood to talk. "And you've had a hysterectomy? When? Why?"

She seemed to struggle to speak. "About ten years ago, for abnormal bleeding. Not cancer. They left the ovaries."

Gary examined her, noting that her scalp was not tender, and that percussion over her sinus did not elicit pain. Examination of her ears, nose and throat were unyielding, and her neck was supple- she could flex readily with no increase in her discomfort. She certainly didn't have the classic "stiff neck" of meningitis. Her lungs were slightly wheezy, probably because she smoked a half-pack of cigarettes a day, despite her diabetes. A sure prescription for early vascular and heart disease, the emergency physician thought. He made a mental note to counsel her at some point, though he didn't feel like broaching the subject just then. He'd found smokers became irritated if he focused more on the smoking early in the encounter, but also that many were receptive if he could make a diagnosis and start therapy, then provide some anti-tobacco teaching.

The abdomen was soft, with tenderness in both lower quadrants. There was no sign of peritoneal irritation, but the tenderness below her umbilicus was significant. Gary decided not to perform a pelvic exam, as there was little to be gained given the prior hysterectomy. Her rectal exam was normal. Her flank regions, overlying the kidneys, were mildly tender to his percussion with a closed fist, but the discomfort was symmetric and suggested sore muscles as much as anything else.

75

"Do you think it's a urine infection?" she asked, anxiously...

He paused for a moment, considering. A short course of antibiotics for cystitis, a bladder infection, in a diabetic, followed by apparent improvement, then a raging febrile illness with abdominal pain. It sure added up to a kidney infection-pyelonephritis. Diabetics seemed to specialize in hiding serious infections, until they became four-plus sick. Normal one minute, then septic and hypotensive the next. It was hard to say exactly why this occurred; even heart attacks could be silent in this population. It might be from dysfunction of the nerve endings, so that pain was not felt normally, a common occurrence in the hands and feet of diabetics. It might also be due to poor immune function, so that normal inflammatory responses were not triggered until later in the illness, as compared to normal patients.

Probably the organism that had infected her bladder was resistant to the amoxicillin or trimethoprim-sulfa that she'd been prescribed, Gary reasoned, or perhaps a virulent strain of the organism had been selected out by the antibiotics themselves. The treatment had been necessary, but the ever-increasing use of antibiotics for minor maladies and nonbacterial infections was a natural pathway to selection of populations of resistant bacteria, and these were becoming more difficult to treat. Now and then, an outbreak of vancomycin-resistant enterococcus, or methicillin-resistant staphylococcus aureus, or even the feared "flesh-eating" streptococcus made its way to the forefront of the news, something that had not happened 20 or 30 years prior, when he'd been entering the profession. Now, populations of healthy, young people suddenly found themselves under assault by aggressive strains of bacteria that had formerly been found only among the immunosuppressed, in institutions. As layer upon layer of antibiotics were created to fight these superbugs, the outbreaks would likelier become nastier and more inevitable. He considered all of this as he pondered what was wrong with this lady, and how he would initiate therapy if infection appeared to be the cause.

"I'd be surprised if it wasn't," he finally replied. "With that high fever, I'm pretty convinced it's a kidney infection, which probably ascended from the bladder infection you just had. We'll collect some urine to send off for culture and a urinalysis, along with some blood. Let me give you something for nausea, and some IV fluids as well. You're bound to be dehydrated."

"OK, doctor," she ascented. Rolling over on the bed, she raised the corner of the washrag that covered her fleshy face and peered out from underneath. "And, can you give me something for this headache?"

"Sure. Let's start with some Tylenol-if we bring down the fever, it will help the headache as well, I think. I'll let the nurses know and someone will be in shortly."

Approaching Karen, he gave her the chart with the orders to be taken off.

"OK, off to the next," he said, turning toward the chart rack.

He began to sense that too many things were happening at one time. Details could easily slip by when it got this busy. During evening shifts, when he split the patient evaluations with a nurse practitioner, it was easy to simply focus on the more serious patients. Though he was required to go over her diagnosis and management plans, her efforts usually saved him a tremendous amount of time. On the night shift, there was no such luxury, and when the department filled up, it was easy to get behind. He gritted his teeth, and hoped for a lull in the action, so that he could catch up.

"Oh-Maryann, we have to get to that pelvic exam," he called out, not really sure of her whereabouts but hoping she could hear him.

She peered out from behind the door of the Gyn room at him, wondering what had taken so long. Apparently, she'd been standing in there for some time, waiting for him.

As he crossed the corridor, Lizzy called out to him suddenly.

"Doctor, I need you down here in room one."

He hurried to the bed, and found the man with the gunshot wounds had become progressively more unstable. He was cool and moist, and his pressure had fallen into the 70's, with a greater elevation of the heart rate.

"The blood, where is it?" he grumbled, looking up at the IV bags.

"I just need to check it; Maryann was going to come in."

"I'll check it-let's just get it up!"

They swiftly confirmed its suitability, and hung the blood with a pressure bag. Rapidly, the man's blood pressure increased into the 100 range. Gary felt a bit of relief. He needed time to get this fellow over to the trauma center. He was silently grateful that it was only five minutes away.

He charged back to the Gyn room. If he could get the gunshot patient out of the department, things would settle down quite a bit, he reasoned, and then he could start dealing with the other, less pressing cases.

"Do you have the cultures swabs and plates, Maryann?" he

asked, closing the door.

"Sure, doctor. Here's the speculum. I warmed it up."

He looked at her and nodded approvingly. Nurses didn't always do that, but it surely made the exam less uncomfortable. It was more evidence of her personal brand of caring.

The young patient looked up indifferently at the ceiling as he seated himself at the foot of the table. He raised up the sheet, exposing her perineum. The Gyn room was a Spartan affair, with little of the décor or warmth that Gary imagined would be present in Gynecologist's office or woman's health center. A large, padded table, with unpleasant-looking metal stirrups that pulled out or retracted, dominated the room; nearby stood a very old, but serviceable, gooseneck lamp. A wheeled stool and a dingy countertop made up the rest of the furnishings.

Gently parting the labial tissues, he guided her through the exam. "OK, some pressure from my fingers, now the speculum."

She shifted uneasily as he pushed the speculum in. Diligently, he searched for the cervix. It wasn't easy to find, as her uterus seemed to be bent into an unusual posterior position, what the gynecologists called "retroverted." It was always embarrassing to malposition the speculum, rooting around to find the appropriate position so that the bottom of the uterus was visible at the far end of the vaginal barrel. Such frustration had been common when he'd been a medical student, and even as a resident he'd fumbled many times. But now, he became angry at himself when he produced this degree of discomfort for a woman, particularly since it was such an awkward exam. After he redirected the speculum a few times, the cervix popped into view. He sensed the woman's impatience, and discomfort.

"Sorry about that. It's finally in good position. Your cervix is kind of red, and there's a lot of thick white discharge coming out of it," he explained.

She was not impressed. "Yeah, that's what they said last time."

"Where do you get your female exams-you know, PAP smears and that?"

He grimaced, as he heard his own question. Not being a native Pittsburgher, he didn't approve of putting "and that" at the end of every other sentence, but it frequently crept into his lexicon.

She shrugged. "I don't really go unless I have a problem. A couple years ago, I went in and everything cleared up after they put me on antibiotics, so I figured I could wait awhile to get

78

checked again."

He removed the speculum, to her relief, and lubricated his gloved fingers.

"Now, two fingers inside," he told her. "I'm going to push on your belly, to feel the uterus and ovaries."

He touched the cervix, straining to get his fingers to it, and moved it gently from side to side.

"Ouch-that's where it hurts! Hold it!" She began moving up the table, away from him.

"Sorry. I don't want to hurt you. When the cervix is that tender, you have an infection. How about the uterus-when I push right here?" he asked, trying to palpate the muscular organ.

"Yeah, that hurts, too. Can you be more gentle?"

Her voice cracked and became higher-pitched. Gary tried to probe more gently.

"I will. And how about on the sides, where your tubes and ovaries are?"

He tried to palpate any enlargement in the ovary or tube that might suggest an abscess, a more significant problem, compared to pelvic inflammatory disease- such a condition would require admission and intravenous antibiotics, possibly even surgical therapy.

"No, not really," she said, easing back onto the table.

"It looks like you've got 'PID' again, you know, an infection of the cervix," he explained to her. "We'll send the cultures, but we need to treat you with antibiotics today." He headed for the door. "I'm still waiting for your urine test. The pregnancy test is negative."

"Thank God," she laughed, relieved at the news, as well as having the exam over with.

The remark was flippant, given the gravity of the situation, and Gary paused.

"But you have to understand, Lori, if you keep getting these infections, you may not ever be able to get pregnant, at least not a normal pregnancy."

At this, the young woman looked concerned, and peered at him inquisitively.

"Didn't anyone ever tell you that?"

She shook her head, and was no longer smiling. "Not that I can remember."

"PID is a really serious health problem. It doesn't just go away. It scars you inside your tubes. That's why we tell people to use condoms for safe sex, and keep your partners to a minimum.

Men can be more careless and not have such severe consequences. A drip, some antibiotics, everything's normal in a week- ready for action. But a woman's reproductive system is much more complicated, and much more prone to internal scarring that can make you infertile forever. It isn't just like a cold or flu you get inside, that goes away when it's treated. These infections scar your tubes. You can get tubal pregnancies much more often, too-and those can be life-threatening. "

The young woman stared sullenly at her naked feet, still in the stirrups, sticking out from beneath the sheet that had been placed over her lower body. She suddenly looked like a little girl to the physician.

"Can you prescribe something for the pain, too?"

"Yes, I will. Why don't we get you into a more comfortable position?" He helped her move back onto the table, getting her feet down.

"Thank you," she said, in a tone that suggested she was really grateful; Gary appreciated that.

He wondered if anyone had ever taken the time to explain anything to this young woman about her reproductive health, or if she'd simply been let to follow the instinctive drive for pleasure. Maybe this time she'd remember, and take pains to protect herself.

It frustrated him that sexual encounters between young people had become as casual as conversation, perhaps even more so, and yet very few of them had a grasp of the implications of pooling their gametes with those of a relative stranger. Maybe it was a failure of the health curriculum in school, or of popular culture, with its "everybody's doing it" message. It was tragic that something so biologically compelling, so completely unavoidable, could be so destructive to young people, with or without the morality baggage. Doubtless physicians had thought the same thing five hundred years earlier, when syphilis and gonorrhea ravaged the population, when genital chancres, painful discharges, spinal cord disease with slap-footed gait, and even brain deterioration with insanity were common sequelae of sexually-transmitted diseases. He shuddered and thought of his own kids. Despite his knowledge, it had not been easy to address these issues with them. He was only too happy to let his wife talk to their daughter about it.

Sometimes, he reflected, the ED was a perfect place to do patient teaching-when people were distressed, they tended to listen- as opposed to the routine "wellness" office visit. But it was

80

at the same time a challenging setting in which to instruct patients: he couldn't spare much time during most shifts to sit and discuss things. The "get 'em in, get 'em out" paradigm that was at the core of the specialty wore on him more than any other aspect of emergency medicine. It was hard to avoid the aura of an assembly line when there was always someone new to see with another problem, and, often, a waiting room full of angry, expectant people.

The woman's boyfriend then slid into the room, glaring contemptuously at Gary with mean, dark eyes. His nose and ears were pierced, and his tank top displayed tan, well-muscled shoulders, covered with faded tattoos. He leaned hard against the wall, and began to speak to his girlfriend in low, gutteral tones that sounded more like snarling than language. His body language suggested ownership of the woman, rather than tenderness or concern. The physician felt sorry for her.

"I'll write all of this down and we'll type it up so you can read it. Then we'll get the antibiotics started and get you going," he offered.

He turned to Joann, who'd been busy labeling the test tubes and petri dishes that they'd utilized. "I'll write orders for the cultures," he told her, preparing to head back out into the ED to see other patients.

"Do you want her to stay till we get the wet prep and yeast smear back?" the nurse asked, scurrying along beside him and placing the specimens on the desktop where the secretary sat, typing into the computer.

"No. We'll just call her if they're positive. I can always call her in a prescription. It takes too long to get them back anymore. I 'm sure it's cost-effective to send them across the river to have them looked at in the lab there, but it's pretty inconvenient."

"Karen-the transfer? What's going on?" he called out, and then leaned over the desk, rubbing his eyes.

"City medics should be here any time."

"Good."

"Maryann," he called. "How are things in there?"

"Pretty much the same, doc. He's still complaining of a lot of pain. But his pressure hasn't really changed."

"And the heart rate?"

"It's up a little. Maybe from his pain..."

"No. He's bleeding. Put up the second unit and call for two more. He needs to go to the OR."

He glanced in at the stricken man, and then walked over to

his bedside.

"How are you, buddy?" the physician asked, taking the man's hand. It was easy to feel close to someone who sensed the severity of his own situation, and who was suffering. He would never have presumed to be so familiar with this young man if he were in the ED under different circumstances, say, for a sprained ankle or cough. This was different. The man might not survive.

"I don't know, doc. It just hurts a lot. You tell me how I'm doing."

His lips were cracked and dry, but he managed a faint smile. He appeared pale, somehow, even with his dark skin. Gary squeezed the man's hand. It was cool and moist. The heart rate hovered at 130. It now took him a few seconds to process the physician's questions and answer them, probably because his brain wasn't receiving an adequate blood supply as his blood pressure fell. He was slipping further into hypovolemic shock, even with blood and crystalloid fluids pouring into him. More volume was the only answer. There were debates in the literature about the merits of treating with massive amounts of blood and fluid to keep the blood pressure normal, when much of the volume simply drained out of the vascular system anyway, wherever the hole was located. But when the patient was showing signs of poor organ perfusion-of shock- the theoretical was less important. Gary knew that he had to replace what was seeping out of the man's vessels.

"Maryann, put a pressure bag on that crystalloid infusion, too. We're still falling behind."

At that moment, two paramedics hurried in with a stretcher. They wore the familiar blue jumpsuits of the Pittsburgh EMS.

Impatiently, Gary briefed the pair, who bustled about, energetically: "you're going to the University. He's looking more shocky every minute. This is his second unit of blood, he's got two big peripheral IV's. I called for more blood, and if it comes in the next couple minutes, you can hang it for the trip over."

"To the ER, over there, doc? Are they expecting us?"

"Yeah. They'll probably have the trauma team waiting as you come in the door. I think he'll get to the OR in short order. Here's the labs and the films. Let me get you the transfer sheet..."

The unit secretary walked it over to them.

"Thanks, Karen. OK, guys: O2, IV's, blood, monitors-let's get him over there!"

The two gingerly picked up the stretcher and moved the unfortunate man, who remained conscious, but who was

82

becoming progressively more confused.

"Doc, his pressure's 100 over 60, but the heart rate is 130. Will you call them with an update for us?" the medic asked.

"Will do. Good luck, sir," he said, again taking the man's moist hand.

The gesture wasn't merely an assessment of the patient's perfusion. The emergency physician had done what he could do in this setting: diagnosed the internal bleeding, sought IV access in multiple places, started fluid and blood under pressure, arranged a transfer. But he was losing. He was worried the man would die in the next few minutes, or in the operating room. As he had gained more experience in his field, he'd become more respectful of human tendencies to touch and comfort injured or dying people. Surely, he thought, as one lay dying, having the hand held or the cheek touched could provide a bit of energy, of soulfulness to support the physiology for just a few more minutes. And let this man know that someone cared as he passed gently into the quiet night.

The medics rushed him out on the gurney, through the glass doors to the waiting ambulance, IV bags swinging wildly about as they loaded him into the rig. Gary watched them for a moment, then hastened back to his remaining patients.

"What about that head CT? Did our fellow go yet?" he asked the secretary.

"No, doc. They've had to call the tech in from home. I just called, and they said he'd be ready in a few minutes."

2a.m.

Two new charts had made their way into the rack, obstacles for Gary to surmount before he could sit down and collect himself. He thought it would be best to check on the old lady with chest pain in bed two, then move to see the new patients. He walked quickly over to her bedside. She was pale, and looked drowsy.

"Mrs. Smith, are you all right?" he addressed her to see how awake she was. "How is your pain?"

She was now barely responsive, and Gary became gravely concerned. He looked at the monitor, and pressed the icon for blood pressure determination. The loud, mechanical sound of the cuff inflating filled the room, and he could see and hear her soft breathing. She'd been in a semi-sitting position, and he hurriedly lay her flat. The blood pressure had fallen to a mere 80 systolic from the 160 that she presented with, and the alarms immediately

83

sounded.

The patient was mumbling something incoherently. There was no longer the flicker of light or of recognition in her eyes. He put a finger on her wrist to check the radial pulse, and lifted her chin to assist her breathing, which had now faltered as her tongue fell backwards to obstruct her airway in the supine position.

"Doctor, I heard the alarms-what happened?" the nurse asked, as she came scurrying in. She took stock of the situation and realized the patient was deteriorating rapidly. "Do you need the intubation tray?"

"I don't know yet, Maryann. Turn the nitroglycerine drip off. That's probably the culprit."

She stopped the infusion of the cardiac medication, while Gary used a syringe to hastily administer fluid, intending to counteract the hypotensive effect of the nitrates. He then cycled the blood pressure cuff again. Within a few seconds, and with some tactile stimulation, the elderly woman began to awaken. Whether this was from improved blood flow to her brain or the attention she was receiving, he wasn't sure. The pressure had rapidly rebounded to 110/62, a much more appropriate state of affairs for a brain in its eighties, Phillips thought.

"Mrs. Janowicz? Are you with me?" he peered into her blue eyes.

The pale face turned to him, and her eyes locked on his, with just a hint of recognition.

"What happened?" she asked, weakly. She turned her head slowly from side to side, attempting to re-gain her orientation, which probably took a lot longer at her age than it would have a few decades earlier.

"Your blood pressure dropped, from the medication we were putting through the IV. I think you're OK now. We'll wait a few minutes and re-set it for a lower dose. How does your chest feel now?"

She looked surprised at the question.

"It's fine, now. I feel much better."

He turned decisively to the nurse. "Let's run it at five micrograms per minute, Maryann. And why don't you get a larger bolus of fluid into her-maybe 300 cc's. Her lungs are clear, and I don't think that that much volume will put her into heart failure. And let's set the monitor to get the pressures every three minutes, at least until we know she'll tolerate the lower dose of nitro."

"OK, doctor- she's up to 110 already," she motioned to the monitor. "I bet she was a little dry. She just couldn't tolerate that

84

much nitroglycerine."

"Right," he replied, relieved that the problem was so easily solved.

"That was a close call," he admitted to himself, and if he'd had enough nursing staff to permit stationing someone at the bedside the entire time she was in the ED, that wouldn't have happened. So be it. Another joy of working the night shift. On daylight, they would have had the manpower to allow closer attention.

He looked steadily at the patient, who lay quietly, observing the proceedings around her. He noted with satisfaction that color had returned to her face. Nitroglycerine was the time-honored therapy for myocardial ischemia, dilating the coronary arteries, improving blood flow to the heart and relaxing the veins throughout the body, which reduced the heart's workload. Unfortunately, it also inevitably dropped the blood pressure, sometimes dangerously. Low blood pressure was dangerous for a lot of reasons. Below some threshold, that was probably different for each individual, the blood flow simply didn't get to crucial beds, and vital organs began to deteriorate, including the brain and heart. Unchecked, the process led to cell injury, release of toxic products from the injured cells, greater vasodilation and a downward spiral towards death. With coronary artery disease, or similar deposits in the arteries of the brain, an obstruction in crucial arteries threatened to reduce flow and produce injury, even in the absence of low blood pressure. When the obstruction was coupled with low pressures, the potential for damage was much higher. Normal perfusion pressures simply had to be maintained in such circumstances.

"Are the enzymes back yet?" he asked.

"No, doctor, Sophie called us from the lab. The lady's blood clotted in the tubes. We had to re-draw her. That second set just went over 15 minutes ago."

Gary scowled.

"Christ! Doesn't this happen all the time? It'll be another half hour at least. This kills me!"

"Y'know," he continued, "she could be having an infarction right before our eyes. I'd really like to see a troponin level. Let's do another EKG, and make sure it's not evolving."

He knew, even as he spoke, that the cardiac blood tests would do little to affect her disposition. The enzymes might be stone-cold normal at the time of the patient's presentation, even if she were having a heart attack. But they were an important part

85

of the presentation, and he wanted to have them before he contacted her attending physician to discuss further therapy, as well as which unit of the hospital she'd be placed in. If they did happen to be elevated, she'd warrant closer observation. The truth was, he could probably begin to arrange her admission even before the cardiac blood tests were back-she certainly wasn't going home. But at night, he just enjoyed complaining about pretty much everything.

Maryann was energetic and upbeat in her response, as usual, ignoring his outburst.

"Sure, doctor, right away."

She wasn't the least offended by his swearing, which he appreciated. After thirty years in nursing, she could probably tolerate anything.

"And let me know when the enzymes are back, Karen," he called, and then repeated, for emphasis, "Let me know when those damned enzymes are back!"

He walked over toward the chart rack and noted that another had been placed there. The first two had been there for the better part of an hour. The diminutive nurse followed him and handed him the repeat EKG from the lady with chest pain. He paused, squinting at the paper. Still the nonspecific changes persisted. And still her heart rate was elevated.

"Even when she's pain free, she's tachycardic," he thought. "What can it be? Pulmonary embolus? But she's not short of breath or hypoxic. Resistant ischemia? But why would she have chest pain one moment, and not the next? Esophagitis from reflux perhaps? Pericarditis? An early manifestation of some infection? A vascular catastrophe, like a leaking aneurysm? An errant gallbladder, presenting with chest pain instead of abdominal pain?" The quandary gnawed at him. He knew that this entity could prove to be anywhere in the spectrum from harmless to deadly, with exactly the same symptoms.

Emergency medicine was often like a mystery novel, he thought. So much of the effort was expended in putting clues together to make the diagnosis, that sometimes deciding on the therapy almost seemed to be secondary. In many cases the diagnosis was not obvious, because signs and symptoms could represent many different disease processes, so everything in emergency medicine was about constructing a reasonable differential diagnosis. That meant weighing all the available facts and listing the possible diagnoses. The treatment plans were usually pretty standard: well-described for the common things, and easy to find in the books or computer for the rare entities that might turn up. But you had to know WHAT you were treating, or all was lost. Treating for the wrong process could lead to wasted time, unnecessary expense, unforeseen side effects, or one of the dreaded, "remember that patient you sent home last night?" conversations.

It all began with the history. People weren't always easy to talk to, especially when the emergency physician had only a minute or two to get the story. Being concerned with his or her own particular circumstances, patients often would meander and digress. It took skill, and tact, to keep a patient on track, while maintaining a sympathetic ear. Some patients would just lie there on the gurney, concentrating on their suffering and providing little history at all-that was an especially difficult situation, and, for Gary, an annoying one. How could he help someone if he didn't know what his symptoms were like? Meanwhile, he had to furiously write down whatever a patient was saying, and begin planning the orders for labs, medications and nursing care that would make things actually happen. The physical exam came next, focused and packed into a few seconds or minutes. Sometimes, he could do both the history and exam at the same time, without appearing to be rushed or officious.

As the data was rapidly assimilated at the bedside, he was already integrating, searching his memory banks, checking his own set of experiences, and generating a list of possible causes. In rank order preference, he would bring a list of potential etiologies to the tip of his temporal lobe, and scrawl the orders that would help verify or exclude the likely choices. Then, quickly, on to the next patient. Sometimes the history and exam revealed an incontrovertible diagnosis, and then laboratory testing was superfluous. In other cases, labs were indispensable.

"Maybe the chest film will tell the tale," he said out loud, referring to the perplexing case of chest pain. He grabbed the film from the jacket, placing it on the viewing box. It was not remarkable.

"No explanation there," he said quietly, looking over the soft tissues, bones, contours of the heart and the vessels and lungs. "No pneumothorax, no widening of the mediastinum, no pleural effusion-nothing . Even the heart size looks normal."

He went through the possibilities again as he walked to the next patient. The evidence supported none of his diagnoses except the failure to get adequate blood flow to the heart, myocardial ischemia-that's what he would have to go with, he decided. In an elderly lady with chest pain that responded to nitroglycerine, with an abnormal EKG and risk factors for atherosclerosis, the probabilities pointed to that diagnosis. As soon as the enzymes came back, he'd place a call to the attending and get her admitted. Admit her on aspirin, nitrates and beta-blockers. Check several sets of serial enzymes to evaluate for cardiac injury, set up a treadmill stress test or a radionuclide perfusion study to assess the integrity of the cardiac vessels, and she'd probably go home in less than 24 hours. Having made his decision, he turned his back on the issue. If new information surfaced, he would re-evaluate. Failing that, the decision was made, the algorithm would be followed. It was time to turn to needs of other patients.

Even if uncertainty remained, it was a relief to settle on a "most probable" diagnosis and DO something. After all, with the exception of glaringly obvious things, like lacerations or broken bones, everything in medicine was a probability game.

Studying the nurse's notes on the chart he had picked up, he walked slowly back toward the "minor" rooms. The angry man with the police was still sounding off, and the air smelled of stale beer as it rang with his ceaseless cursing. Gary walked into the room next to the prisoner and introduced himself to an 18 year old, slight man whose hazel eyes were glassy and distant. He had a mop of dark hair that stuck out in multiple directions, in a most peculiar fashion.

"Hello," Phillips said, "are you Terry Englert?"

The man nodded blankly.

"It says you hurt your finger-what happened?"

He held up a swollen, deformed right ring finger. No verbal response to the question was forthcoming. Gary ground his teeth together. Apparently, this wasn't going to be easy.

"That looks painful-how'd you do it?" he asked, trying to sound sympathetic.

The young man looked at his friend who sat on a chair in the exam room, smirking. This room, too, smelled of alcohol, and Gary sensed his patience dwindling as the two snickered to each other.

"Well, it's a long story..." the boy began, laughing as he spoke.

"Can you give me the short version? We have to get that thing X-rayed and treated. Did you punch something, or fall or what?"

Again, the man eyed his friend, grinning impishly.

"You might say that, Doc. I guess I was trying to punch my

friend, and I fell down at the same time. I don't really know what I hit. But I did a helluva job," he waved the finger in the air demonstrably.

Gently taking the man's injured hand, Gary began to examine the ring finger. There was swelling and ecchymosis about the first knuckle. It appeared deformed and somewhat rotated. He flexed and extended the distal knuckle, which the man resisted.

"Owww! Dude-don't touch it!" he cried out, pulling his finger away abruptly.

The doctor sighed and looked up, expecting angry eye contact. Instead, the young man was again looking at his friend. Noting the deformity, the physician thought about the possibilities. This could be a fracture, but it looked partially dislocated, too. He doubted whether any mere soft tissue disruption would produce so much swelling.

"Sorry," the physician said aloud, releasing the man's hand. "I do have to look at it at some point. Let's get the films, and then I'll examine you more closely."

"How long will that take?"

"What?"

"The films, dude. How long?" the kid demanded.

"Probably a half hour. I've got a lot of customers to take care of tonight. I can't promise it any sooner," he retorted, expressing the best-case scenario. It would likely be closer to an hour, perhaps more. He figured if these two were drunk or high, they could entertain each other with their silliness to pass the time- it really shouldn't matter too much to them.

"OK, but make it fast. We've gotta get out of here soon."

"What the hell did you come here for? Does your health matter less to you than your next social engagement?" the physician thought, angrily. Gary hated being put on notice that someone was in a hurry. Wasn't everyone in a hurry? He could sense his tolerance slipping away. Disgusted, he headed back toward the nursing station.

"Hey, doc. This hurts, you know. How about a pain pill or something?"

"OK, sure. I'll send it right in," he mumbled on his way back to the chart rack. Two more to see, then maybe I can get people moving, he thought.

"Lizzie, can you take this guy in six an ibuprofen? 600 milligrams, please." No one seemed to hear him, except the patient.

"Motrin? That's bullshit," he heard the kid say, probably

89

with the intention of being overheard.

"OK," murmured Gary. "Maybe it's bullshit. But when you come in after drinking, you get bullshit for pain. I'm not gonna get you high on oxycodone right now."

Alcohol and pain medications didn't mix well, and in extreme cases could cause coma, or at least respiratory depression. He didn't have the nursing personnel to stand guard over the man, watching for bad things that might or might not occur. Better to deal with drunken dissatisfaction, he reminded himself.

He turned to find Karen patiently waiting for him.

"Doc, I've got your enzymes-they look normal." She handed him the printout, as he picked up a new chart.

Again he paced over to the elderly lady in bed 2. She looked much better than when she'd come in. Actually, he noted with a degree of satisfaction, she looked pretty comfortable.

"How's your pain now, Mrs. Smith?" he said to her, though she was dozing.

She started, and turned her head towards him. "Oh, doctor, I'm sorry. I nodded off. I do feel a lot better. I think I'm back to normal. Thank you."

"But is that pain you came in with gone? Are you comfortable?"

She nodded, putting her hand on her chest. "Yes, I think so. I don't feel any pain at all right now."

He looked at the monitor behind her. Her blood pressure was fine, but the heart rate hadn't budged.

"I hate tachycardia," he repeated to himself.

He felt defeated. It was an inevitable aspect of emergency medicine that sometimes there just wasn't a ready explanation for the signs and symptoms with which patients presented. But it was perhaps a small consolation to recognize that the patient had at least the potential for serious illness, and then take steps to protect him or her. He looked longingly at the chair, unoccupied, which sat beside Karen. Then he turned to look down at the chart he'd just picked up.

"Weakness," read the chief complaint.

It was such a nonspecific symptom. Surely, he figured, they could elicit a little more useful information out front, when they signed the patient in to the ED. Anyway, eliciting specific information was his job, and it didn't usually take too many questions to focus in on one organ system or another. He approached the room, and suddenly found himself facing the brother of the man who had been brought for his headache and inability to care for himself.

"Doctor, what's happening with Bartholomew?" the man asked, an edge of impatience in his voice.

"Sir, I'm waiting for someone to come down from the psychiatry floor to help me sort this out. And, I'm awaiting his lab tests. In the meantime, we're just trying to keep him comfortable."

"OK, doctor. I appreciate your efforts. I just don't think we can manage him at home anymore. He's lived with my mother all his life, but she's over eighty and she just had a colostomy. She can barely care for herself, and I don't have room for him in my little house."

The man repeated the whole story, as though he was afraid that Gary had forgotten the gravity of the situation. Still, he was respectful and polite, which was reason enough to try to get his wishes fulfilled.

"We'll see what we can do, sir."

The physician actually had no idea what he would do with Bartholomew, who seemed mentally deficient and not the least bit acutely ill. He hoped the psych consultant would admit him and work out the social issues.

Stepping into the exam room of his next patient, he was taken aback by the complexion of the elderly man who lay in the bed, smiling pleasantly. He was absolutely white. Even his lips had a ghastly pallor. Gary took the man's hand, and, impressed by the firmness of his handshake, introduced himself.

"Mr. Krapczyk, what's the matter? You look like a ghost! How long have you been so pale?" He spoke with some levity, though he knew immediately that the problem was a serious one.

A small, stout woman, sitting primly in the only chair in the room, answered for him.

"Doctor, he's been pale for weeks. It's getting worse, and tonight he got dizzy. I had to half-carry him up the stairs myself. But he couldn't stand up on his own, even when I got him up there. I called a neighbor to come help and we brought him down to the emergency right away. I called Dr. Taylor, but he said we better come on down to the hospital. Is he here?"

"No, ma'am. I'm the only doctor here right now. Usually, I see the patients in the emergency room for the primary doctors, then call them to let them know what I've found, and then we discuss treatment. Just from looking at him, I'm sure we'll be keeping Mr. Krapczyk in the hospital. Has he been having any dark stools or blood in the stools?"

The man answered, cocking his head to the side. He chose his words carefully and deliberately, making certain that he was well understood. The emergency physician later learned that the man had been a civil engineer before he retired, perhaps explaining a tendency toward precision.

"Oh, yes. My stools have been kind of dark probably for the past four weeks. Do you think that's part of the problem?"

"It might be. We'll check it out."

Examining the man as he spoke with him, Gary took note of his pale conjunctiva and his skin color, though the rest of his physical exam was benign. The rectal exam was remarkable for charcoal-consistency stool which was strongly positive for blood when he checked it with a hemoccult card. Blood lost slowly in the upper GI tract undergoes a degradation process in the bowel that results in a dark color, and a change in its makeup, he reminded himself, resulting in the so-called "tarry" stool. Occult blood loss via this route could become very dangerous before it was discovered. Apparently, the man had been losing blood from the GI tract for weeks or months, and his anemia had finally stopped him in his tracks. It was a common turn of events in the elderly.

There were other considerations for the differential diagnosis of anemia, besides loss of blood from the body, more insidious ones. Gary quizzed himself on the potential etiologies of the anemia. Blood cells could be destroyed within the vascular system, a process called hemolysis, due to a variety of different mechanisms, including immune cell dysfunction, a spleen gone awry, attack by errant antibodies, or blood-borne malignancies like leukemia. Or, the bone marrow might fail to keep up with the production of new red blood cells, due to tumor replacement of the marrow, or inadequate intake of certain nutrients necessary for blood cell production, such as vitamin B12. All of these could result in anemia, at times profound. But the clinical evidence in this case strongly supported lower GI bleeding in this man, and Gary would proceed accordingly.

The nurses had already put an IV in and drawn the lab tests in the elderly man, while his energetic little wife watched on, approvingly. It was clear that he would need blood, and Gary wrote orders for a second IV to be placed, in case of the need for vigorous fluid resuscitation; he also arranged for a type and crossmatch for four units of blood, and routine laboratory studies. Just from looking at his severe degree of pallor, the emergency physician figured the man's hemoglobin would be about seven. He also ordered a liter of normal saline solution to go into the IV quickly, to address the marginal blood pressure, while they waited for the blood to be prepared. Unfortunately, the man would also need a nasogastric tube placed through his nose and down into the stomach to make sure he wasn't bleeding from an ulcer in that area, one of the possible causes of this sort of blood loss.

"Allright, sir. Plan to stay with us, and I'm sure we'll be giving you some blood tonight. Meantime, we'll get some fluid into you, and check your blood counts. I'll give Dr. Taylor a call as soon as I get some results."

The man grumbled weakly, a mock protest for the benefit of his wife. He knew full well that he could not continue at home with this degree of anemia. The affectionate lady pulled her chair up as close to the bed as she could maneuver it, and patted her husband's hand, then entwined the fingers with her own. There was a sense of great strength about her, and Gary figured that the man's support system was about as favorable as it could be.

Exiting the room, he returned to the chart rack, and grabbed one of the blue clipboards. Now, just one chart remained in the "to be seen" rack. He began to hope he could clear things out and lay down for a half hour before dawn. It never seemed to work that way, though. People trickled in all night, at precisely the rate needed to make sure he could never have a moment to catch his breath or rest. Ten minutes after he put his head down, the phone would inevitably ring. That extraordinarily short moment of dozing actually seemed to make his exhaustion worse, and contributed to a strange sense of disorientation that could take quite a while to clear.

"Tooth pain" was listed as the chief complaint on the chart. He walked down the hall slowly, and as an afterthought, called over his shoulder to the secretary, who sat blankly in front of her computer screen. Even Karen was susceptible to the doldrums at these early hours, if there was no stimulation.

"Uh, Karen, could you ask Maryann to get me another EKG in room two? And go ahead and call Dr. Swanson for me. It'll take him an hour to call back at this time of night."

Some of the PCPs were on the phone, returning calls, in a matter of a few minutes. Others, more difficult to rouse, could take quite a while to return the call.

Most of the patients who came in complaining of dental pain were middle-aged or young people who smoked and drank and seldom brushed. There was typically a mixture of tooth decay, chronic gum disease, acute gum inflammation or even abscess, and a characteristic odor of dying tissue. In the majority of them,

93

he would find multiple brown, rancid nubbins of former teeth that barely projected above an angry red gum line.

"Morning Miss Czezarch-did I say that right?" He immediately affirmed his suspicion-the smell of tobacco was very prominent as soon as he crossed the threshold into the room. The patient was a pretty, plethoric lady in her mid 40's, with a kindly manner. Even though she was suffering she seemed to maintain a bright outlook and a bit of a sense of humor. Interacting with such gracious patients provided him with a real sense of worth.

"Carol, just call me Carol. Doc, my mouth is killing me. Can ya' tell?"

She immediately opened her mouth to reveal the yellow, stained remnants of her molars, which were more like stumps than teeth at this stage. She pointed to the upper right jaw. The tooth she indicated looked like all the others: discolored, hollowed-out and badly in need of removal. Her gums were likewise in terrible shape, receding and swollen. They looked friable and sensitive.

"It looks bad all right. Is your face swollen?" He stepped back and squinted at her, trying to compare the two sides of her face.

"Yeah, it's puffy here, on the right cheek, right over where it hurts." she said, gesturing again to her right jaw. The area was a bit swollen, and perhaps reddened. Her face was smooth and round to begin with. The protruding cheek now helped to fashion that side of her head into a hemisphere, and if the other side had been involved, it would have been very close to perfectly round, Gary thought.

Examining her diligently, the discerning physician tapped gently over the maxillary bone, above her mouth on the right.

"Yes, yes that's it." she pulled her head back away from him, grimacing.

"Sorry, Carol. I'm sure your tooth is behind all this, but your sinus could be infected, too. I think it's worth an X-ray."

"Can you give me something for pain, doc? I been in agony all night tonight." Her face reflected her suffering, as she grimaced for emphasis.

He folded his arms, regarding her with mock formality.

"I'm happy to give you a pain pill, and a prescription for pain meds and antibiotics. But I also want to do a nerve block on that tooth."

"You mean stick a needle in it? Awww, Doc, no way-it's killing me." She waved her arms wildly, as if fighting off an enemy

94

that was attacking her with a sharp object.

"But it will relieve your pain, in just a couple minutes!"

"I'll take my chances," she said, firmly.

"Well, let's just start with the film. We'll talk about the nerve block again when it comes back."

He moved back to the nurses' station, recording his exam. The dental problem certainly seemed legitimate. Gary often wondered how often such people with chronically bad teeth stopped in for a convenient pain pill prescription, but then ignored the problem until the next toothache came. They all knew that he, as an emergency doc, was unlikely to pull their teeth, so why wait till three in the morning and then make it an issue? It was a chronic complaint among the physicians in his group, but they all knew the answer. The dentists weren't available at three a.m., almost none of them did charity work, and most patients didn't show up at the dental school for free care until there was no choice in the matter.

Such behavior often raised the suspicions of docs and nurses in the ED. But every time he branded a patient a "drug-seeker" in his mind, nagging doubts crept in. What if he was wrong? Could he really send someone out on ibuprofen if it did little for his or her pain? So much of the diagnosis and treatment rested on the patient history- it was all so subjective! You could read it in any of the medical texts-people have vastly different pain perceptions, pain thresholds and responses to treatment. In this vast sea of medical uncertainty, how could he be sure if a patient was putting on, or was in real pain? Better to err on the side of patient advocacy, and treat, he'd always reasoned. It occasionally met with the scorn of nurses or colleagues, but he could live with that. He'd often check the patient's willingness to tolerate a nerve block as a "test" of the severity of the suffering, presuming that anyone who wouldn't go for it really didn't have very much pain. But he was aware of the limitations. Some people were so needle-phobic that they'd endure days of a toothache rather than have a needle stuck in the gums.

Ambling back to the nursing station, he sat down to collect himself and catch up on paperwork. Reclining at the cubicle that was reserved for the physician on duty, he felt exhaustion overwhelm him. He put his head forward into his hands, and for a moment, he lapsed into unconsciousness. The pleasant interlude was quickly interrupted.

"Doc, sorry to startle you, but that fellow with the facial injury is back from his head CT," Karen said, touching him gently on the shoulder.

"Right!" he said, abruptly.

His head snapped up, and he was instantly ready to deal with the problems at hand. "Set me up a suture tray, with something for irrigation and some 6-0 nylon. I wear seven gloves, not seven-and-a-half. I'll get some lidocaine and we'll get the ball rolling."

He looked longingly at the remaining chart in the rack, then at the clock. The shift was not yet half over, and he felt profoundly exhausted. He'd begun to regard every night shift as a major challenge. It was never quiet anymore, the way it had been on some nights when he'd first started, nearly two decades prior. And the staffing was marginal for these higher numbers: One doc and two nurses just didn't cut it when things were really hopping. That issue should have been addressed long before now, he thought. He could use another nurse most of the time, no doubt about that. But nobody wanted to take that step, especially now, with the hospital on the verge of some major transformation. It was challenging enough to keep the night nurses they had, someone had once pointed out to him. And where would the money come from? Operating margins kept shrinking for little hospitals like this one, and the payer mix in the ED seemed to be getting worse.

The phone rang, and the secretary quickly handed it to him. "It's the radiologist, doc."

He listened as the radiology physician on duty over at the university described the facial fracture of the left maxilla and the orbital floor. There was no intracranial injury, no brain injury, no blood collection.

"Do we need to get specific sinus cuts?" he asked.

"I doubt it. If the surgeon wants them we can always get them later. Just have them call us to arrange it, if need be," came the reply.

Gary agreed, and set off to repair the laceration.

"South Side Hospital, this is medic eight," the radio suddenly came to life. He stopped in mid-stride, walking back to the radio, which was situated on his desk. He grimaced as he waited for a second call.

Again the radio squawked, filled with static but unmistakably calling for his ED.

He picked up the handset to talk to the medics in the field. "Go ahead, Medic 8, this is South Side."

"We're inbound to your facility with a 94 year old female who fell out of bed at her personal care home. Staff states that she's been falling a lot lately, and tonight she stumbled trying to go to the bathroom. She has a history of dementia, CHF and breast CA, and also two prior TIA's. Her vital signs are stable, and be advised we'll be at your facility in five minutes. We've attempted an IV twice, and placed her on high flow O2. Blood pressure is 190/100, her heart rate is 76, in sinus rhythm on the monitor and respiratory rate is 20 with SaO2 of 99%. Any questions or orders?"

Squinting, he tried to picture the patient while the medics continued the report.

"The patient fell and injured her head, and she has a laceration over her right eyebrow. Also, she's complaining of left hip pain. Her leg is externally rotated. We have her in C-spine precautions and fully immobilized. We'll be at your door in about four minutes."

He declined to intervene-it sounded as though they had the bases covered. "No orders, we'll see you at the bedside momentarily."

He liked to meet the medics inside the assigned treatment room when he could, to get the complete story from the source directly, rather than trying to decipher the triage note from the nurses. He told Joann to meet the medics in room one as soon as they arrived.

"It doesn't sound too emergent," he thought, "a laceration and a hip fracture. Treatable problems. I'm still way behind on the paperwork for the rest of these people-I'll let Maryann do the triage, and get the story from her."

He began to fill out some of the history and physical sheets he'd left undone in the flurry of activity earlier.

"Ah, yes," he reminded himself. "I need to sew up that guy's face."

After filling out a few of the forms for patient exams, he got up and walked back to the exam room. The gentleman who'd been injured in the melee at the bar lay on the bed in handcuffs, blood crusted over his face and down the front of his shirt, despite the makeshift bandage the nurses had placed on his arrival. At least the bleeding had stopped.

"Mr. Gorvosky, good news and bad news. The good news is that your brain is not injured-the CT scan showed everything intact up there. The bad news is that fracture of the cheekbone. It may need surgery, I'm afraid."

The man looked even more depressed, if that was possible, after this news. He looked up at Gary with his intact eye, and suddenly reacted to the fact that the injured globe could not move, creating a disturbing double vision. He put his hand over the dysfunctional eye.

"That's just freakin' great. So what do we do tonight?"

"I'll sew up your laceration. Then we get this little legal matter taken care of, and I arrange care for your fracture."

The man shrugged, and looked at the policeman, dejectedly.

"I'll get started on the laceration while I wait for the facial surgeon to call me. Meanwhile, I'll run in some IV antibiotics since your sinus is involved. This kind of fracture can cause an infection, especially with the involvement of the sinus, which can have bacteria in it."

Gary eased the patient back on the stretcher and began to irrigate the laceration over the man's cheek. It looked clean enough but it was badly contused and the edges didn't look good. These blows to the face, with resultant splitting of the tissues from shear blunt force, made for the ugliest wounds. The skin essentially had burst apart. They never looked as good as he'd have liked after they were sewn, and they inevitably scarred in a much uglier fashion than lacerations from sharp objects. Sometimes, patients requested plastic surgeons to perform this type of closure, but not if they'd been drinking-that group just didn't care. Actually, he thought, it would have been pretty convenient to have a plastics consultation on a busy night like this-it would have freed him up from a half hour of closing the laceration, which he could have used. But no such request was forthcoming from the patient. Nothing would be simple this night.

"OWW! Hey what is that?" the patient squirmed with pain as the impatient physician began to inject the local anesthetic, using a small syringe and a very fine needle. The needle was seldom painful, but the solution could produce a brief, severe burning sensation.

"Pinch and burn, sir," he said, intent on his work.

The man breathed heavily as the rest of the lidocaine was injected.

"What am I gonna do now?" He asked in a feeble voice.

Gary sighed to himself, as the predictable psychotherapy session began. He hated this part: he didn't really mind being a counselor, but in these circumstances, the patient was usually seriously intoxicated, and the counseling was either useless or quickly forgotten. He ended up saying the same things to the unfortunate patient over and over again.

"Well, for the first part, you've got to cut down on your

drinking," he commented, inserting the first suture through the ragged wound edge.

"I only drink on weekends," the man objected.

At least he seemed to be listening, Gary observed, surprised. "Yeah, but a half a case at one time is too much!"

He was guessing, but the man had certainly had imbibed more than the "two beers" that most patients claimed to have imbibed when they arrived in the ED.

"My girlfriend hates it when I lose my temper-I'm gonna be in so much trouble," he confided.

"She'll get over it, if she really cares for you. And if you listen to me and cut your drinking, these temper tantrums can stop."

"Yeah, I gotta cut down, I know it..."

Gary wondered for a second if the man was going to ask to be admitted for detoxification from alcohol, a direction he didn't want to go right now. No one would seriously entertain the request until a patient was completely sober, so the man would then have to spend the night in the ED, before any real progress could be made along those lines.

"I don't have any money, anyway. How am I gonna pay for this? These doctor bills are outrageous. I got my fist cut up last year in a fight, and it got infected. They took me to Mercy and I had to go to the operating room to get it cleaned out. I *still* haven't paid for that one."

"Are you working?" the physician asked. He was afraid the answer would be "no," which made the possibility of coping with these debts very slim.

"Kinda. You know, odd jobs and construction."

"No insurance?"

"No. My boss laughed at me last year when I asked about insurance coverage. Then he laid me off two months later anyway. They'd take a half of my paycheck for insurance if I paid it myself. I gotta pay the rent and my truck payments."

"I see your point. But the hospital will accept some payment. Even if it's a few bucks a month. You know, like a payment plan. At least it'll keep your credit clean."

The man grunted his assent, and settled into a quiet reverie for a moment. Gary wondered if he'd gone to sleep. He drew the skin together carefully. His tired eyes found it hard to coordinate grabbing the fine suture and pulling it through the knots he created. As always, the needle driver was inferior in quality, a hand-me-down from the OR, after the surgeons found that it was no longer acceptable.

"I don't have any money," the man suddenly blurted out again. "How am I going to pay for this?" He didn't remember the conversation they'd had just a few minutes before.

"Trust me, things will work out somehow," Gary answered, gently. "but you have to quit drinking, friend, or your entire life will collapse."

He pulled the sterile drapes off the man's face and sat for a moment, looking at him. "It's remarkable," he thought, "that I can speak to a voice under that towel, sewing up a gash without seeing the man's face, and remain entirely detached, as though he weren't a person at all. I felt no pity for him while we talked, none whatsoever. But take off the drapes, and there is his tortured and melancholy expression again. His lot in life is terrible, at least right now... The ED can be such a depressing place to work-all of society's ills and malfeasance manifest here, eventually. The drunkenness, the rape, the abuse, the assault, the drugs, the depression, the suicide, the psychoses...mix in all of the naturally-occurring infirmities and you have a miniature hell on earth. We civilize it, of course, with crisp white linens, and flushing toilets; intravenous infusions and drugs for any malady known or described. But God, on some nights, I wonder if I really help anyone at all? Or is it just window dressing and band-aids?"

Stepping back, he looked upon the man's bruised, beaten face. His thoughts became more cynical.

"Do six stitches in this guy's face make a damn bit of difference in his life?" he inquired of himself, silently. "I doubt it. The laceration will heal faster, and maybe is less likely to get infected. His scar will be smaller, as if he really cares. But did I make any impact at all on the one process that's gonna kill him-this year or next, or in five years? No. He won't remember one thing I said about drinking. As soon as he's out of jail, probably tonight, he'll go to bed, wake up hung over, and think about the next time and place he'll get drunk. And after a fight, or a loss of consciousness, or a fall with another laceration, he'll be in here again, or another ED..."

"I'll get his instructions typed up and you can get down to the jail," Gary told the policeman, who was sitting silently, with his arms folded. The patient had fallen asleep again, oblivious to his condition or his destination.

"Here, Lizzie," he called, catching a glimpse of her by the computer where she could type up the discharge instructions.

"I'll write up a script clearing him for jail. He just needs a

100

bandage and some antibiotic ointment. By the way, did you update his tetanus? And a referral to the University ENT clinic for that fracture. We can call tomorrow and coordinate a follow up, then call him, wherever he'll be."

Once or twice on a night shift, when the department wasn't coming apart beneath him, Gary felt the need to step outside, just for a few minutes. The nurses understood; they could retrieve him within 15 seconds or so. He simply had to step away from the phone calls, the interruptions, the charting, and let his mind experience a short respite. Behind the hospital, between the back walls and the elevated railway bed, there was an alleyway. Here, he stood on sultry summer nights, and sometimes on frigid winter ones, ensconced by the darkness and briefly entranced by his short-lived freedom.

He usually used these interludes to smoke a cigarette, a mortal sin of which he was deeply ashamed but somehow unable to extirpate. Nicotine had been a delightful source of energy and verve when he was in college; in medical school he'd been convinced to give it up...almost. The profound dependence that he'd developed had never completely given way to his conscious desire, and, thirty years later, he was still subject to the aching desire for a cigarette, especially when things became frenetic in the department. At home, he never bothered, except for an occasional cigar on the weekends. But something about the high-grade psychological demands of the ED made nicotine an imperative, if he could get to it.

He took a deep draught of the night air. It was thick and close, its humidity laden with scents-creasote from the rail line above, a faint whiff of honeysuckle growing up near the tracks, and an acrid, metallic smell. He recognized the latter well-it was literally the smell of iron in the air. He'd grown up with it. Pittsburgh had been not only been subject to inversions of the smoke that spewed from its metal mills and foundries, but also to the essence of the very products that they created. The city smelled like the minerals of the earth that had given it a reason for being. To the southeast, along the Monongahela, the furnaces of the Edgar Thompson works were rendering steel from iron ore and coke. The lone operating steel mill in the city still made its presence known.

Once, when his grandmother had spent a week in the South Side hospital, courtesy of her inflamed gall bladder, Gary remembered coming to visit her, and walking to the family lounge with his cousin, while the adults chatted aimlessly. The large windows on the fourth floor overlooked the entire South Side, and the mills were in full swing, then. The two watched, enthralled, as short trains hauled by switch engines paraded cars through the streets just below them, servicing the tall, brick brewery buildings. Beyond, they looked over row after row of modest townhouses, and could see the dark, expansive mills crowded near the river. Black and foreboding, lights pierced the skylights of their roofs in places, and the tall, imposing towers of the blast furnaces were alight with the flames shooting from their own stacks. The mills were the axis around which the city revolved-this was apparent even to the two pubescent boys. An uncle toiled there, a great-uncle had been crippled there, their grandfather unloaded railroad cars in service to the men who worked there, the brewery supplied the libations that allowed for relief and recreation among the millworkers. And young friends aspired to join the generations who had made the mills function morning, noon and night. For the two innocents, the "iron city" felt, tasted and smelled of metallurgy. When those stimuli once again wafted upon the languid breezes of the summer night, Gary knew the city, knew more about it than he could ever have articulated.

The wall against which he'd been leaning began to vibrate, and he heard the air horns of an approaching train piercing the thick night air, reverberating through the entire river basin. The dynamism of the massive locomotives never failed to thrill him, and he looked at the top of the nearby trestle, hoping to catch a glimpse of the diesel's headlights as it rumbled by. The long freights used to haul in uncountable loads of raw materials for synthesis into the building blocks of the world here in Pittsburgh; now, they mostly seemed headed for someplace else, laden with cars and pickups made with steel that had been fabricated in some far-flung corner of the earth.

"Doctor. Doctor Phillips!"

It was Karen. There was a phone call. The respites were always too brief, but he was deeply grateful for them. He snuffed his cigarette against the black stones of the retaining wall, and walked back to the department.

Slipping in the side door, he grabbed a handful of lab papers off of the printer, he looked them over. The lady with abdominal pain and probable UTI had an elevated white blood cell count. Most everything else was normal. Including her urine. That was a surprise to the exhausted physician, and he clenched his teeth in frustration.

"I've gotta look somewhere else for the source of this fever, but where?" He wondered aloud. "She's got a mild cough, probably from smoking, but it's probably worth checking a chest X-ray. If that's clear, maybe I'd better do an abdominal CT-she's pretty tender in the lower quadrants. Could be an abscess, I suppose, from diverticulitis. Or perhaps a colitis."

"Karen, can you get a chest X-ray on the lady in six for me? I'll go let her know." He headed towards her room, enumerating the possible causes of her fever.

3a.m.

At this point, he saw flashing lights reflected in the ambulance entrance door.

"Medics are here," Joann called cheerfully.

Gary sat wearily down and began looking at paperwork, figuring out which patients he could provide a disposition for at this point.

"Let's see, room 2, still waiting for her attending to call, and I need to write orders. Room 4 is waiting for amylase/lipase levels, room 5 needs an X-ray of the finger, room 6 needs a film of her sinuses. And 7 is discharged to jail. The fellow dropped off by his brother is stable, waiting for psych, the lady in 6 hasn't had her chest film yet, and I need a hemoglobin level on the fellow with the GI bleed. I'll eyeball the new patient and get back to see the patient in 9. Then maybe I can start some admission orders for a few of these people."

He leaned back heavily in his chair. Once, this had all seemed so appealing: the acuity, the variety, the flow from one case to another, the hard-edge interface with the street. As a medical student, and later as a resident, he had delighted in moving rapidly from bedside to bedside, intervening quickly in one situation after the next as fast as he could scribble orders and spit out a dictation. It did not matter that lives were in shambles, that human misery was the constant companion of the "great case." There was such excitement in exploring a ragged wound, in seeking a foreign body, in packing a nosebleed, in opening an abscess. And the more invasive the procedure, the more he and his colleagues-in-training had longed to perform them: the residents touted them to one another, wore them like medals or decorations. They described their feats with the utmost bravado. Placing a chest tube, putting in a jugular venous line, intubating the trachea, reducing a dislocated joint: all were applied to treat life- or limb-threatening problems, and it was immensely

103

satisfying to perform these maneuvers, for both oneself and for the patient.

But somehow, 20 years into the profession, he had become weary of the treadmill. His interaction with patients was so often methodical, focused, to the point. There was little time to ask who the patients were, what they did, where they were from. Each was but a case, a chief complaint, to be quickly examined, evaluated and treated, with disposition rapidly to follow. He had entered a humanitarian field, only to find that he had precious little time for the humans.

Sometimes, when it wasn't so busy, or when he was on his way home, he would fantasize about a different way of life. Patients would come to see him in his office, sitting in front of his mahogany desk while he spoke to them from a comfortable leather chair. He would regard them with kindness and patience. There would be the necessary medical questions, and, in the exam room, a physical. But he would speak to them, really speak to them, about their lives. And some would come back to see him again and again. They would treat him as a concerned old friend, not an intruder, walking in on them at a vulnerable moment of suffering. Some would bring him brownies, or cookies. He listened with envy sometimes as friends from medical school who had become primary care providers discussed their practices, relating how this or that patient had brought them tokens of esteem and gratitude. It wasn't something he experienced very often.

In recent years, he began to hear talk about "burnout" among his emergency medicine colleagues. There didn't seem to be very many old emergency physicians, at least not that Gary knew personally. But he didn't feel burned out, so much as he felt empty or hollow. He had no time to relate to the people he treated, or their families. They seldom came back, unless they took a turn for the worse, which elicited in him only a sense of disappointment or failure. Somewhere, inside himself, he simply needed to know and understand these patients he served. Basic human interaction frequently eluded him, in a sea of human misery. The profession was a noble one, and he was proud he'd chosen it. But as his autumn years approached, he felt a yearning for fewer "great cases" and many more great people.

There were options, he knew. Emergency medicine doctors were talented generalists. Primary care, perhaps for an HMO, might be possible, or he could retrain in something less acute, like industrial medicine, or toxicology. But he was getting older quickly, and the thought of change was intimidating.

"Doc, can you come in here, please," Maryann called, interrupting his pensive moment, with some urgency in her voice. That couldn't be good.

He dropped the papers he had been working on and walked over to the room.

One of the medics from the rig that had just pulled up addressed him as he entered. "Doc, she just went out on us. She was mumbling and talking the whole way here in the back of the rig. Then, right when we pulled in, she stopped. She's just kinda snoring now."

He was a young paramedic, with a crop of blond hair that stuck up in the air. He spoke rapidly, unnerved by what had happened to the old woman so unpredictably.

"Yeah, so I see. Karen," he bellowed to the secretary, outside, "call respiratory. Let's set up to intubate her-how old is she again? Does she have a living will?"

"We don't know. They didn't send one from the home, if she does."

"Karen, call this nursing home, quick. Find out if she has a living will or any limitations to therapy." He dropped his voice. "She may not be long for this world; let's make sure we act by her wishes."

"Can you get me an intubation tray, Maryann? And the airway drug box. Let's just assist her ventilation with the bag-mask for now, until the respiratory tech gets here and we get an answer about this living will. She's got a bit of a gag reflex but it's pretty feeble."

He rubbed her breastbone vigorously, to which the elderly lady grimaced and moaned. Checking her pupils, he found both to be irregular and immobile, with evidence of prior surgery for cataracts. They were no help at all in his diagnostic evaluation. She seemed not to move her left arm, and barely moved her left leg. Her twisted, wrinkled face made it difficult to tell if her facial muscles were weak or not. The tongue lay in the midline, but she followed no commands, simply moaning to an uncomfortable stimulus. She did not localize a painful stimulus with her left hand, indicating a more profound neurologic insult, or a deeper degree of coma.

Gary listened to her lungs and heart, and evaluated the cut on her scalp, which appeared minor. As always, after a fall, the patient had been placed on a backboard and a hard cervical collar placed to protect the neck. This might make visualization of her

105

airway for intubation all the more difficult, but there was no way to be certain that this lady had not injured her neck or spinal cord when she fell. Manipulating the bones of her neck, while trying to place a breathing tube in her trachea could turn her into a paraplegic, as if things weren't already bad enough. There wasn't time to get the full set of X-rays to "clear" the spine, and a ligament injury wouldn't show up on the plane films, anyway. So he would have to manage the airway with a presumption of neck injury, having one of the nurses immobilize her head and neck while he placed the tube into her airway. He turned his attention to her chest cage, abdomen and pelvis. All appeared uninjured. Her abdomen bore the scars of many prior surgeries, but it was soft. Her extremities were thin to the point of being skeletal, and gnarled with degenerative arthritis, as befit a 90 year old. Her left foot was externally rotated, and that leg appeared shortened compared to the other.

"It looks like she fractured her hip, too," the emergency physician said, quietly.

"Doctor, I talked to the nurse supervisor at the nursing home. She has no family, and no living will."

"That's a shame," the emergency physician thought. "She's probably at the end of her life. I bet she stroked, got confused, tried to get up and then fell, breaking the hip. What a tragedy. It looks like she has a pretty dense hemiplegia, and she's probably aphasic, too, judging by her responses. I doubt that she will ever speak or walk again. That on top of her preexisting Alzheimer's disease."

"Well," he said, "let's get her airway protected, then get a CT and some neck films, along with the pelvis and hip."

"Do you think she bled into her brain?" asked Maryanne.

"I don't," he answered, curtly.

"It's probably an ischemic stroke, from a clot or atherosclerosis. I guess she could've hit her head and bled but the head injury looks pretty minor. Still, I've been fooled by subdural hematomas before. The 'bridging veins' inside our heads get pretty fragile as we get old."

"Well, doctor, mine are getting more fragile all the time," the sprightly nurse quipped, as she began to undress the patient and obtain her vital signs.

"Mine, too. Especially after nights like this," Gary acknowledged, and smiled at her. There were few moments of levity this night, but he was grateful for this one. Nurses were such important comrades-in-arms for difficult cases. He was glad to

106

have the rapport he had with this team. A few others he'd worked with had not been so helpful nor so collegial. A physician sometimes had the sense of driving the nurses and techs mercilessly, to the point of exhaustion, but it was all dictated by patient care. Things had to get done, the pace had to be maintained, or they'd all be overwhelmed by the sheer numbers of patients and tasks required to take care of them.

"Let me scribble some orders for Karen. Call for the head CT, please."

He grabbed an order sheet and hastily wrote down his orders.

"Respiratory is here," Karen called. The respiratory therapist literally ran into the department, panting.

"Hi, Eddie. Will you assist her ventilation the while we get the tools and drugs ready? This lady likely has had a stroke and can't protect her airway. I also need someone to do cricoid pressure, and that."

It was an incontrovertible fact of emergency medicine: patients in coma, or with neurologic compromise, couldn't protect their own airway, even if they appeared to be breathing without a problem. Left on their own, there was too much risk of airway obstruction from their own tongue and pharyngeal tissues, as well as the possibility that any stomach contents that refluxed up into the throat-all too common in sick people-would find its way into the airway and cause a life-threatening aspiration pneumonia. Therefore, the physician needed to protect the airway with an endotracheal tube, in a process called intubation. In order to make certain that the patient was not conscious for this unpleasant event, and to ensure the best view of the airway, drugs were administered to provide a deep level of anesthesia and relaxation of the muscles.

"OK, Maryanne," he continued, "Have you got etomidate and succinylcholine? On second thought, who knows whether she's had a preexisting neurologic deficit? Let's go with rocuronium for the relaxant. That'll make it easy to get a CT afterwards, anyway. And, I'll need some midazolam and fentanyl to keep her sedated for the next hour, because she'll be paralyzed for quite a while."

Gary then made his way to the top of the bed, carefully arraying his tools for the intubation. The suction worked well, the laryngoscope light was fine, the endotracheal tube had a stylet. He asked Lizzy to stabilize the neck while he removed the collar, demonstrating to her how to keep it in a neutral position as he tried to place the tracheal tube. She reminded him tersely that she'd done that particular task before. He looked at the patient's vital signs. The oxygen saturation, which had been in the low 90's on arrival, was now 100%, thanks to Eddie's assistance with the bag-and-mask. They'd pre-oxygenated her as best they could, in order to assure a reservoir of the precious gas in the lungs during the period of tube placement, since no gas exchange could occur for that period.

"I'm ready. Push the drugs now, please. Don't forget the cricoid pressure, Eddie. Stop assisting her breathing now, please."

The respiratory therapist put the bag aside, concentrating on the anterior neck pressure, which was supposed to help prevent regurgitation during these vulnerable few moments.

Gary opened the patient's mouth, pushing the tongue aside with the blade of the laryngoscope. He followed the tongue carefully, looking for the flap of tissue at its base, the epiglottis, which would lead him directly to the opening of the airway.

"There's a lot of thick mucus back here," he said aloud, to no one in particular. Someone handed him a tonsil sucker.

"Let me suck it out-OK, good view of the cords."

Since residency, he'd habitually described whatever he saw in the back of the throat. In those days, the attending physician wanted to know what the resident saw, so that he could have confidence in the tube placement- or, if there was uncertainty, he could take over, brushing the trainee aside and placing the tube himself. Gary pushed the tube between the vocal cords and the patient gave a weak coughing motion, despite the muscle relaxant she'd been given. That was a good confirmatory sign.

"Pull the stylet out now, please. Take a listen for me, and let's see some CO_2. There's the color change." He was satisfied that the tube was in the right place. "Eddie, can you fix this tube in place for me?"

He heaved a sigh of relief as the therapist began to stabilize the tube with a device that looked a little like the faceguard from a football helmet. Difficult intubations were unusual, but when they happened, things got chaotic quickly. This one had been pretty routine, fortunately, and the emergency physician was pleased for the moment.

Stepping back, he folded his arms, really looking at the patient for the first time. She was creased and wrinkled, like one of those apple sculptures that people put in the oven, he thought. Her eyes were a dull, far off kind of blue, and there had been no recognition that another human was talking to her. A victim of senile dementia, and now a dense stroke, Gary felt an aching sadness as he looked at her. It was unlikely, he mused, that she would ever again have a quality interaction with another person. Could she contribute meaningfully to a discussion, a game or even a hug? And where was her family, the last level of caring for so many of the elderly? Perhaps all of them had moved away, or perhaps she'd been a spinster, with no offspring. The alternative, that relatives were out there, but that no one much cared what happened to her, was more painful to consider. Perhaps in the morning relatives would come to her bedside.

"And now," he thought, looking at her immobile form, rhythmically inflated by a mechanical ventilator, "she's on a machine that keeps her alive. Maybe she'll return to independent breathing, maybe not." The risk of an acquired hospital infection was now much higher than it had been just ten minutes before. If she couldn't wean off the ventilator, it would mean a tracheostomy tube had to be inserted into her neck with a surgical procedure, in a week or so. She would descend further and further into the maelstrom of modern medical care, wherein each small decision about machines, or antibiotics, or transfusion, represented a domino in a long line of dominoes, each tipping into the next until the chain of medical events took on a life of its own. With no one to speak for her, no one to say "enough!" the dominoes would continue to fall, until her feeble constitution permitted recovery, which was unlikely, or until infection or complications killed her. He hoped that family members would intervene on her behalf should her course become so hopeless.

No wonder so many nurses, young and old, joked that they'd one day get a tattoo on the chest, which read "Do not resuscitate." Death with peace and dignity seemed so rare in the hospital, despite the capacity to make the end serene and tolerable. It was especially problematic when no one could come forward to speak in the patient's interest, or relate what she would have wanted.

He recalled once presiding over a "terminal wean" in a patient with no chance for recovery after a neurologic catastrophe, as a senior resident in the ICU. He had supervised the administration of morphine by drip as the patient was extubated, and death was certain. In essence, they'd quelled the patient's suffering while the family held his hand, weeping but satisfied to be present at the end. No gasping, no choking, just peace. Gary hoped for such an end.

"OK, she's got muscle relaxation for the CT, anyway," he said quietly. "She should be still for the study. Eddie, can you get me a blood gas in half an hour? She'll be back in the department by then."

The therapist nodded as he adjusted the alarms on the ventilator.

"Her blood pressure is coming down, doctor-what would you like me to do?" the nurse asked, a note of concern in her voice.

"Maryanne, I think this is the usual after intubation-you know, the positive pressure in the chest reduces the return of venous blood to the heart, and stroke volume and blood pressure fall. Just give her a fluid bolus- start with 300 cc's normal saline. And let's see what happens. I think she'll go back to her baseline. We should at least keep the systolic over 140, where she started. We need a decent pressure head to perfuse the brain in the face of this stroke."

"Doctor?" Karen poked her head into the room.

"I've got Dr. Peters on the phone, about the lady in room 3."

"OK, great." He went to the phone, and, picking it up, described the patient and her course to the sleepy attending.

"I wrote orders to admit her to step down and rule her out for MI...sure, I'll get her on a beta blocker-I already started it here in the ED. And I'll add low molecular weight heparin, and put in a consult to cardiology."

He began scribbling more orders below those he'd written. The heparin would reduce clotting tendencies, hopefully keeping the coronary arteries open and avoiding a heart attack, or minimizing the extent of one that might be occurring.

"By the way," Lizzie called, "what are you going to do with that man with the belly pain? I think everything's back on him."

"Oh, good. And how is his pain?"

"A bit better. He dozed off a little while ago."

"Let me look over his labs, here. Uh-huh. His white count is up. And his lipase is three thousand. Pretty much what we thought-pancreatitis. His transaminase levels are up some, as well, probably from the effect of his imbibing on the liver."

He pulled out another order sheet. "Who's on call for general medicine?"

Karen looked crossly over her reading glasses at him.

"It's William John."

"Oh, no," Gary shook his head, grumbling. "Not him. Every time I call him to admit someone, he gives me nine yards of shit. And he always wants to pan it off on somebody else. Are you sure there aren't any old records on this guy? Maybe there's a prior

110

admission to somebody else."

"No. I called down to medical records. There aren't any old inpatient records."

"And you're sure he listed no attending physician?"

"Real sure. He lives on the street. If he had a doctor he probably couldn't remember who it was, anyway. I think we're stuck with Dr. John."

"God. Allright, page him for me. Let's see how this goes."

"And, those finger films are back for the guy back in eight," she added, deftly pushing at the numbers on the phone.

"OK, I'll go check them out. Did we ever get those sinus films, on the lady with tooth pain? And how about the chest X-ray on our lady with fever?"

Stifling a yawn, he grabbed the film jackets and put the finger films up on the view box. At last, it felt like he was moving things along. Maybe he could get all of these patients treated and dispositioned before dawn, after all. With luck, he imagined, he could lie down for just a few minutes. It never seemed to happen, but he never stopped hoping for it, either.

Studying the X-rays with bloodshot eyes, he commented aloud to himself. "I guess I shouldn't be too surprised-he's dislocated the PIP joint. And it looks like a small avulsion fracture, as well. I'll block his finger and put it back in place, and get him on his way."

He then turned his attention to the febrile woman's film. "Hmmm... the lady's chest is clear. I should have known. Now what? I need to reexamine her belly."

"Doc," Karen interrupted. "I have the hemoglobin level for you on Mr. Krapczyk. It's not pretty."

He turned to her, not interested in guessing.

"It's only 5. 3!"

"Wow. Well, he looks like a friendly ghost for good reason. Have them send us two units of packed red blood cells to transfuse. Let's get his attending on the phone, too. It's Taylor."

"Mrs. Hammersmith," he approached the woman with fever and abdominal pain. "I need to look at you again."

She squinted, looking very miserable. Shifting from her side to her back, she grimaced and moaned as he palpated her lower abdomen.

"The chest film is clear. I still have no reason for this high fever and the pain. It could be diverticulitis or an abscess. You're tender enough that we need to consider it-I'm going to order a CT scan of the abdomen and pelvis."

She nodded, silently. He'd hoped that with fluids, acetaminophen and time, she'd feel better. But the fever hadn't broken, and she was as uncomfortable as when she'd come in. He needed to expand his search. This wasn't a "surgical" belly, at least not a classic one, but she could be hiding a pus pocket.

"Ma'am, let's get you some medication for the pain, while we're working on finding out what's causing it-we'll put some Dilaudid through your IV. It usually works well, but it can make you drowsy."

Moving to the med room, Gary drew up a syringe of plain lidocaine, a local anesthetic, for the young man with the dislocated finger. This kid was a little flaky, already, he thought. How is he going to handle a digital block? A needle inserted at the base of his finger on both sides? It might be asking a bit much.

He walked in, brandishing the syringe.

"Whoa, is that for me, man?" the young man cringed on the table. "I don't do needles, doc. Just put it back in place and I'll be on my way."

Gary frowned. "I barely looked at you and you nearly jumped off the table. Now you want me to snap a dislocation back in place without numbing your finger? I don't think that's gonna work out very well. Anyway, you're covered with tattoos-don't they use needles down at the Tattoo Emporium? How'd you sit through that if you have such a fear of needles?"

Sometimes, the irritable physician reminded himself, you could shame reticent young men into accepting injections if you reminded them that their tattoos required dozens of needle-sticks. It didn't always work.

"I'm serious, doc! Needles scare the hell outta me!" He looked imploringly at his silent, smirking friend.

"Just get the damn shot, already. We been here an hour, and we got places to go," the companion suddenly said, dismissively.

He heard a commotion out at the desk. Karen began calling him, not certain of where he'd gone to.

"Doctor-they need you in the CT scan. That lady is seizing, or something."

"Great," he muttered. "Look, I'll be right back. Think this over and we'll get it done. The needle hurts for about 30 seconds, then you get numb. We'll splint it afterwards, and I'll write you a script for some pain pills. That's it-then you're out of here."

He didn't wait to hear the response, and ran out of the department, around the corner to the long empty corridors of radiology.

112

"Amber, what's going on?" he asked the technician, a tall, affable blonde woman, who appeared anxious and uncertain.

"I think she was taking a seizure. She just began to shake all over. For about a half a minute. Now she's calmed down."

He turned to the nursing supervisor, who'd been sent to accompany the patient to radiology, since the ER staff was so busy.

"I'm not sure if it was a seizure, but she did shake all over," she said. "Her saturations never dropped. I hadn't seen any voluntary motion before this occurred. She seems to be breathing all right now. Let me cycle the blood pressure cuff again."

Gary pressed firmly on the patient's nailbed, and she moved her right hand.

"The rocuronium is wearing off. She's no longer relaxed. That's fine. Anyway, we can monitor her neurologic status more effectively."

At this point, the doctor noted several jerky, irregular twitching motions of the right hand. It did not appear volitional.

"I think she might be starting to seize again," he said. "Can you give her two milligrams of Ativan IV? That should settle her down. How is the CT scan coming?"

"We were finishing," the tech said. "I just sent the images to the radiologist-she should be calling you shortly."

"OK-let me run through them, too-at least I can look for a bleed or any sign of high ICP."

The technician displayed the cuts on the monitor as Gary looked at each in turn. The various lobes of the brain were shrunken, the folds enhanced. He looked for any areas of significant enhancement to suggest acute bleeding into or around the brain.

"I don't see anything but old, atrophic brain. No fracture. No bleed. Send her back over now, and I'll work on an ICU admission."

He walked back into the department just as a disheveled man was walking from the triage area toward the exam rooms, following Lizzy, who led in her usual, spirited fashion. The man dragged his feet reluctantly, and kept his head down constantly. Gary darted by the two, preparing again to convince the man with the dislocated finger to submit to a finger block.

"Doc, I've got the radiologist on the phone, and so is Dr. John." Karen spent most of her night tracking down the emergency physician as he moved from bed to bed, trying to connect him to other physicians.

He shook his head, reversing his course. "It will be a miracle if I can do even one thing tonight without an interruption," he thought. Karen handed him the phone, wincing as he grabbed it with frustration.

"William. Hi-I have a patient here for you who needs to be admitted. Nice fellow who drinks a bit. Got himself a raging case of pancreatitis, I'm afraid. Can I go ahead and write admission orders for you-IV fluids, bowel rest, pain meds, alcohol withdrawal precautions?"

He cocked his head, irritated by the mere thought of the forthcoming response.

"Here it comes", he thought as he was greeted with a pause on the other end of the phone. He listened to the other's protestations.

"No, Bill," he replied, sourly. "The GI service will not admit a man with pancreatitis. They seldom admit anyone, let alone a patient with an assigned PCP from the ED, who could consult them. No, I don't think any of the surgeons will admit him, either. This fellow is gonna have to be on your service..."

He hesitated, grating his teeth, listening to the various excuses offered on the other end.

"Bill, even if you are going out of town, someone has to cover your service. You probably shouldn't be on call if you're going out of town. More to the point, you shouldn't be going out of town if you're on call. Who's covering for you while you go away?"

The secretary smirked and shook her head as she watched Gary playing the game with the elusive PCP.

"OK, I'll call him." The emergency physician backed down, abruptly hanging up the phone.

"You see, Karen, you see! He always gives me grief. Why does he stay on the call list when he never wants to be called?"

"Maybe," she said, "maybe it's an insurance issue..."

"But it's always an insurance issue with him. All of his patients are in Medicaid HMO's, which pay just about nothing. His practice can't be profitable-I don't know how he stays afloat. But it *is* his practice, and his choice.

"Can you tell me what line the radiologist is on?" he asked, changing the subject.

"She hung up, I'm afraid."

"Shit. Can you call her back? It's four a.m. Everybody wants to crawl back into bed. I don't blame her."

A loud voice distracted him, as looked down in dismay.

"Dude, I'm outta here!" the man with the dislocated finger

114

shouted angrily, walking out of his room and towards the door. His silent, skulking friend shadowed him, leering at the staff.

"Hey, wait," the physician called. "I'm coming right back to block that finger and put it back."

"No way, dude. You had your chance an hour ago. I been here way too long. I told you we had places to go, and that."

"Well, I tried to fix it a half hour ago and you wouldn't let me. You can't leave that joint out of place-it will never heal."

"I don't wait, doc. I'll stick a splint on it or something."

The frazzled physician considered his options as the intoxicated pair walked away.

"At least let me put a splint on it. And you need to sign out against medical advice."

"Uh-uh. I'm not signing anything," he countered. The friend glowered at Gary.

"Well-if you can't wait while I tend to an emergency, I can't help that. But you're welcome to come back tomorrow. It may hurt a lot more," the physician added.

"No way, man. I'll go across the river, to Mercy. They treat you with respect, there."

"Yes, I'm sure they do. Just make sure you get the finger taken care of. The longer you wait, the worse chance you have for normal healing or good function, bud." Gary sat down with a sigh.

The two young men let loose a stream of profanity as they exited, mixed with degrading statements about the ER and its staff. The kid had been drinking, but he wasn't nuts or psychotic. In America, Phillips reasoned, people can walk out and refuse treatment, even under the influence. He'd written a note on the chart to document the exchange, and there had been witnesses. Whether this would protect him from a lawsuit if things went badly was uncertain. The hospital would consider this an "elopement" and he'd have to explain it, and justify it, to someone, who would in turn have to report it to the state department of health, in a monthly summary. But, he wondered, would it be appropriate to block the kid's exit, deeming him incapable of making decisions because of the beer he'd drunk? A purist might say "yes." However, forcing him back into his room, having security hold him until he sobered up, seemed more like kidnapping than anything in the best interest of the patient. Such elopements by angry, drunken patients were common, and they were a gray area. When was a patient who'd indulged in alcohol no longer capable of making a reasonable decision? Gary thought that, if a patient understood the nature of the injury, could speak

115

and ambulate, and made a conscious decision to leave despite being told that it could have deleterious consequences, it was probably reasonable to let him go. Still, he was pretty sure that a good attorney could make him look foolish and careless for adopting such a stance.

"That's just great, huh, Karen?" Gary asked as he approached the secretary's perch in the center of the ED. He was becoming exhausted, and interactions like that just made him feel depressed.

Karen put her head in her hands, rubbing her round, oily face.

"Every night, a parade of abusive people. Don't take it personally, doc. You always take these sign-outs so hard. It just comes with the territory. Drunk, high people are not nice. They don't care about themselves, they don't care about us. Why get worked up? He'll be back tomorrow when his finger is killin' him. Or, he'll go to Mercy. He won't pay anyone a dime, anyway. If things don't go well, he'll try to sue somebody. I doubt if that will get very far, given his behavior. If they're interested, you take care of 'em. If not, move on to the next. Your plate's full enough anyway right now, isn't it? And, a year from now, if we're shut down, who's gonna care, anyway?"

"Doctor, our lady is starting to drop her pressure again." It was Joann, calling from room one. Though generally indefatigable, even she was starting to look tired.

Lizzy bellied up behind him. "I just put a depressed guy back in room 8. He's a drug addict who fell off the wagon. He wants to detox. And there's another new patient back in fast track who has pain when he urinates. He's a little hard to understand-he may have a drip."

"Great. We don't have detox here. Call the psych nurse down to help arrange inpatient therapy for him, will you? I don't have an hour to call around to a bunch of hospitals. And we still need them to help us with that guy brought in for disposition by his brother. His labs were all normal. They'll probably need to admit him and work on placement."

"I did call them. They can't come down for a while-you know they need the nursing supervisor to fill in while they do consults down here. And she's been tied up over in CT with that lady with the stroke."

He looked at the charts in the rack, in various stages of completeness, wishing it were morning and that he could go to sleep. Without speaking, he rose and walked into room one, looking at the elderly woman who was now struggling on the ventilator, protesting against each breath the machine delivered. Joann was busy at the bedside. The diminutive woman's blood pressure was still not as high as he would have liked.

"Why don't we change her to an IMV setting? Let's have her breathe some on her own. Maybe she'll tolerate that a bit better. If that doesn't work, call Eddie and we'll go with pressure support. Meantime, let's give her another fluid bolus-250 cc's of normal saline. She looked pretty dry to start with. See if that bumps the pressure. If not, we'll stick in a central line and start dopamine at a low rate."

"OK, doctor. We'll call respiratory, and I'll open the fluids. Do you want to give anything to calm her down?"

"I don't know, Joann. I'm afraid of dropping the pressure further. She might be restless from pain, or confusion, or bladder distension, or just being on the vent. Let's try to get better synchrony with the machine, first. Try to talk to her and calm her down. Put a catheter in her bladder, too, if she doesn't already have one. Are there any relatives we could call?"

"The home said there was no one but a son in California, who's never been to visit her since the day she came in, two years ago."

Karen called out to them, "Doc, I have the radiologist on the line for you-"

He moved quickly to the desk.

"Hi, Jackie. Sorry to wake you. Do you see anything on this head CT-I did not."

The radiologist described only the appearance of old brain and some chronic changes consistent with lacunar infarcts, tiny strokes, in the left occipital region, probably silent in this patient, but possibly contributing to her dementia. A pretty standard set of findings in such an elderly patient.

"OK, thanks."

Gary recited the management plan aloud to himself. "Ischemic stroke. Keep her a little dry, avoid secondary brain insult, maintain a reasonable blood pressure, treat infection or fever aggressively, and start her on platelet inhibitors."

"Karen, get me Dr. Abrams so we can get an ICU bed for her. And, call respiratory down for us, too. Oh, yeah, and then I need Rogers, the GI guy, not the pulmonologist-but I'm afraid he won't admit the patient with pancreatitis. He'll probably refer me to someone else. And, I still have to get a look at those sinus X-rays."

"Now," he thought, "back to that fellow in the fast track."

He found a middle-aged man lying on his side, sleeping soundly on the exam table.

"Sir...Mr. Negabayu? It's me, Dr. Phillips. Sorry to take so long. What can I do for you tonight?"

The man sat up, rubbing his eyes. He looked sleepy, and a little confused. He had very dark skin, nearly ebony, which made his eyes look starkly white, even though the sclera were muddied by age. He indicated his pubic region with his right hand. He made a gesture that Gary interpreted as referring to urination.

"Right here...hurts. Pain when I ..."

His English was broken and his accent thick. From Africa, Gary surmised. He had trouble understanding the patient, but the likelihood of getting a translator from whatever country on that continent that the man called home was essentially nil in the middle of the night. He didn't even know what language the man spoke.

"It says you went to the doctor for this problem just last week, here on the chart," the physician said, hoping to derive more information.

"He give medicine...still burns."

He made the universal gesture for urine flow, accompanied by a swishing sound to indicate a stream of water. Now, the physician understood.

"I see. OK. I will now examine you..."

Gary spoke slowly and emphatically, hoping that his message would be understood. He began to examine the man. His blood pressure was elevated, and he was rather overweight. His lower abdomen was not particularly tender. Examining the genitals, he found no masses or tenderness, nor was there any evidence of urethral discharge.

"I expect you probably have a urine infection. We'll need to get a urine specimen. I ought to check your kidney function with blood tests, too." He tried to enunciate clearly, and performed a pantomime at the same time, indicating urine flow, and a blood draw.

The man shrugged. Gary wondered if the patient understood any of what he'd said. It didn't make a lot of sense that he would still have symptoms of a UTI after a week on antibiotics, unless it was caused by a resistant bacteria, or perhaps if it had settled in his kidneys or prostate. He made a mental note to come back and perform a rectal exam so he could palpate the prostate gland, later. "That ought to be a treat," he thought, anticipating

118

his difficulty in explaining what he was going to do.

Placing the new set of orders on the desk in front of Karen, he went back to see the lady with the toothache.

"Uh, Carol?" he nudged the dozing woman gently on the shoulder.

"What? What?" she was immediately awake, blinking at him, trying to orient herself to the unfamiliar surroundings.

"Carol, it's me, Dr. Phillips-remember? Your X-rays look normal. I don't see any sinus infection. So I'm going to get you on some antibiotics, and some pain medication."

She nodded, drowsily, but reached up and caressed the sore area on her face.

"And now, let's talk about that nerve block, again."

"No, please, doc. No needles. I'll just go with the prescriptions, if that's OK."

He shrugged, too weary to contest the issue.

"Well, we'll make sure you have the number for the university dental clinic-they'll take care of you there. Call them first thing in the morning. They'll probably tell you to come in tomorrow afternoon. Don't sit on this, or you could get a very serious facial abscess."

She agreed, and he wrote the prescriptions as he walked back to the desk. It was momentarily satisfying to put the chart in the discharge rack.

The phone rang, the characteristic double ring of an outside call. It was the PCP for the patient who'd suffered a stroke. Gary quickly picked up, anxious to get a disposition on the unfortunate patient, and get her up to the ICU. He did not have the nursing manpower to deal with this critically ill patient for much longer.

"Hello, Ralph. I'm sorry to call you at such an early hour, but I have one of your patients, here, who suffered a CVA, fell out of bed and apparently fractured her hip. The brain CT is normal. Her neck films are OK except for arthritis, but she's basically unresponsive so we'll keep her in the collar until she wakes up or we can get a CT of the cervical spine. She was at baseline pretty demented, and now is severely aphasic. I had to protect her airway, and she's on the ventilator. I'll put her in the ICU, and consult neurology, and physical therapy, along with pulmonary to take care of her respiratory issues. I'm not sure if she can swallow-we'll probably need the speech therapist to see her after she's extubated. I'll keep her in traction for her hip, and consult orthopedics."

He hung up the phone. "Joanne, could you get a 325 mg

aspirin, also?"

"For you, doctor, or the patient?"

"Ha, ha," he laughed sarcastically. "For the lady in one. I guess she can't take it by mouth, so give her a suppository."

4a.m.

Looking at the rack, he glared at the one remaining chart, as if it were his personal enemy. It was all that stood between him and the feeling of well-being that came with being caught up. He began to grouse to himself about the delays that were always encountered in the middle of the night. "When are the psych people coming down? And, why do psych patients always decompensate in the middle of the night?"

Gary ambled grudgingly back to room eight, chart in hand. Inside, there sat a dysphoric man who slumped forward in his chair, like a disheveled, weather beaten rag doll. He was middle-aged in looks and spirit, but only 35 years old according to his chart. His hair was scant and thin, already graying about the temples.

"Mr. Anderson?"

"Yeah. Oh, good morning doctor.

"I'm Doctor Phillips-what can we do for you today?"

The man looked at his feet, moist and foul-smelling in old, wretched sneakers. His eyes remained downcast, even when he spoke.

"I gotta get off these drugs, doc."

"What are you using?"

"Heroin, and sometimes crack." He stared fixedly down, not moving.

"Have you been through detox before?"

"Yeah. A couple times. I got clean for three months last time. But two weeks ago a friend of mine offered me some heroin-that's all it took. It's killin' me doc. I'm depressed and I wish I was dead."

The man already looked devoid of life. When he did look up, he couldn't make eye contact. His eyes were a dull, slate gray that reminded Phillips of the hull of a warship. The face had no expression-not even sadness could be detected in the drooping, apathetic eyelids or the indifferent mouth that hid his tobacco-stained teeth. His skin was a sallow, unhealthy tone-not quite jaundiced, nor ruddy, nor pale, just a sick sort of color. In his upbeat, intoxicated youth he'd apparently invested in a variety of

120

tattoos of ferocious animals and near-naked women that now clung to his flesh precariously, reminders of his vacuous existence.

"You really look depressed," the physician offered, stating the obvious in an attempt to show his sympathy.

"I'm so depressed I wish I wasn't here anymore." Tears glistened in the man's eyes.

Gary knew that the man knew that stating his suicidal ideation would get him in the hospital-somewhere, anyway. He didn't doubt his sincerity, but patients who'd been in and out of psychiatric facilities were well aware of how to express themselves to meet the requirements for admission. Now it would be a game-would the hospital psychiatrist on-call accept the patient for admission? Was the man in the correct catchment area? If the psychiatrist wouldn't take the admission, where would he have to go? How long would the poor fellow sit in the ER before he began to threaten that he would like to leave? And would he simply try to elope, so that security had to restrain him? It was all so predictable, he thought. He had watched this man and his kindred spirits glide through the ER and the mental health system hundreds of times. Whatever successes there were would not be visible to him-only the countless failures, who came back again and again, more broken down each time, more pathetic with each visit. The merry-go-round spun on.

"As you know, sir, I'm the medical doctor. My job is to make sure there's no medical emergency here. Do you have any medical problems?"

"Uh... I think I have hepatitis. You know, from shooting drugs."

"Yeah, that's unfortunately very common. A real hazard of IV drugs. What type of hepatitis do you have?"

"I'm not sure," he mumbled.

"Who diagnosed it?" the physician asked, warily.

"They told me a couple years ago, when I was in for detox."

"That's it? No treatment? No follow up?"

"I was supposed to go over to the liver clinic at the University. I felt OK after detox, so I never went."

"That's not good. Once you get admitted, we can get the records. Meantime, let's just check your liver function testes and enzymes to see how things are now. Can you give us blood and a urine sample?

"Yeah," he replied, "I guess so. Do you have anything I could eat?"

"We do. The nurse will get you a bag lunch. Let me examine

you first."

Gary had the man lay down on the table and inspected him. His eyes did look mildly jaundiced, he thought. The liver was not enlarged, though. Probably scarred. There was no peripheral edema, but he did have a lot of plump, spidery-looking veins on his legs and abdomen, likely evidence of cirrhosis, harbingers of the dangerously elevated pressures in the blood vessels that coursed through his scarred liver, now dilated and tortuous. Those inside his esophagus and stomach were likely to look the same, waiting for some minor trauma to produce a massive upper gastrointestinal bleed. The patient remained silent during the exam, following commands dutifully. It was hard not to feel depressed along with him. His life seemed to have been completely destroyed by the drugs and alcohol he had indulged in.

"OK, I'll call the folks from the psych floor to get working on this detox issue," he said as he left the room.

Silently, Gary was thankful for the assiduous psych nurses, who would now spend hours trying to find a place for this patient to go. He felt sure that the man's age and track record would lead the psychiatrists at the South Side hospital to reject him. This sort of problem was not the reason he'd chosen to practice emergency medicine, but the man needed care as much as someone with a heart attack. To street him or ignore his pleas might lead to a suicide attempt.

"I guess I better get a tox screen and liver profile," he mused. "I'm sure they'll ask for it as part of the medical clearance."

Sitting down, he began shuffling through the papers that had accumulated on his desk, and soon his head drooped forward. It was well after 4:00, and soon it would be light outside. He'd abandoned any hope of getting sleep this night. When the dawn crept through the ambulance doors, it would be easier to function, and his brain would emerge from the nebulous cloud of exhaustion he found himself in.

As he sat, in a sleepy haze, he thought of his call nights in residency, minding the patients on the wards, or in the critical care units. Many times he'd been up all night, on the internal medicine service, then shuffled to the morning report early the next day, where senior residents would grill him over one medical decision or the next. On the surgical services and in the ICU, he'd start rounding at 5a.m. to present the patients to an impatient attending physician two hours later.

He remembered, tucked away in a dark corner of his mind,

how often he felt a profound depression in that witching hour as the dawn lay just out of reach. Frequently, he would imagine himself dead, found lifeless by a friend, or hit by a car and suddenly deceased. It was a perverse neuro-psychiatric reaction to his fatigue and sleep deprivation, but in those moments he couldn't see past the murky depths of his deep depression. There was no therapy except for the ending of the 36-hour call day and a night's sleep. Then, a couple of days later, he'd be on call again, and the cycle would repeat. The measure of time in training was based on call shifts; he'd made his way through the months by counting the ones gone by, and the ones yet to come.

It had once seemed noble and admirable to work tirelessly through the night, the weary physician thought, trying to help the ill and suffering. Now sometimes it just seemed stupid, something to be avoided at all costs. Many sleepless nights over the years had changed his perspective. Somehow, it had become difficult to see the resultant good of his hours of toil and frustration. And on some nights, it merely seemed futile. The parade of ill and suffering people did not end, would never end.

When he dozed, late at night, he would sometime see before him images of the patients who had done poorly under his care: the man with severe, new onset pancreatitis, who had turned out to have an infarcted bowel, and who died the next day, just as the true diagnosis was discovered...the baby with bilateral bacterial knee infections who presented too late to save the bone, and who probably would never walk in his lifetime...the chain smoking Vietnamese lady with an apparent lung mass, who turned out to instead have a thoracic aortic aneurysm, dying the next morning before her CT scan could reveal the correct diagnosis... the former, well-known professional football player who was brought to the ER in cardiac arrest, never to be revived...a young, nameless girl who'd taken massive quantities of her antidepressant and whose heart simply gave up in front of him, despite frantic efforts to resuscitate her.

Each time he was overcome with exhaustion and depression on the edge of the dawn, these images would materialize before him. His life as a physician had not been a failure-many people had been helped, lives had been saved, much suffering ameliorated. But the patients that represented his failures, whether from his stupidity, or his inexperience or a disorder he couldn't treat-these would haunt him, he was sure, until he died himself. And, to be certain, there would be more. There was no escape from bad outcomes in medical practice-a physician could only struggle to minimize them.

Again his light sleep was interrupted by the annoying crackling of the radio.

"South Side hospital, this is Medic 8."

He glared at the medic phone. "Why now?" He thought, angrily. "Can I not get a minute of peace?"

"South Side, do you read?"

He picked up the receiver reluctantly.

"Go ahead, Medic 8. This is South Side."

"We are inbound to your facility with a 33 year old male found unconscious by his friends at a party. The patient is a heroin user. We found him unresponsive and barely breathing at the scene. Respiratory rate at that time was only six per minute. We mask ventilated him and obtained IV access, then gave the patient two milligrams of naloxone. He awoke immediately, and is now awake and oriented, with strong respirations and clear breath sounds. The saturation is 97%. He denies any chest pain or shortness of breath. His other vital signs are currently normal. Any orders?"

"No further orders, Medic 8. See you at the bedside."

"That's confirmed. We should be at your door in eight minutes."

Gary scowled in the general direction of the secretary, who appeared as if she'd been dozing herself. Very few presentations of this nature were likely to earn his sympathy at this time of the night.

"Let's hope," he said, "that this guy is looking for his coat and hat when he gets here. Now, Karen, let's see. Where are we with the CT of the abdomen? And do I have blood to hang on the guy in room 4 yet? As soon as I do, I'll call his attending and get him admitted."

A large figure suddenly loomed across the desk in front of him, and Phillips was acutely aware of the smell of an unwashed body.

"Hi, doctor. I have an infection in my armpit again."

"Hi, Lisa."

Gary suddenly had to smile. Lisa was a "frequent flyer," a lady who loved to come to the ED, whatever the reason. She was intellectually slow, but kind, and very dramatic.

"Just let the nurse take you back to your room and I'll be in to see you."

"OK, doctor," she announced loudly enough for everyone in the emergency room to hear her. "I tried to squeeze it myself, and

I got some pus out, and it smelled really bad. But then it festered again and got even bigger. I think you need to lance it and give me antibiotics."

He folded his arms and looked at her.

"Sounds like you've got it all figured out, Lisa. Are you sure you even need me?"

She grinned, revealing her broad, toothy smile. "Of course I need you. You've got to cut it open and get all the pus out."

Lisa came in almost weekly for one thing or another. Her abscesses were one issue, and problems with her feet were another. Her hygiene was poor, probably contributing to both problems. But over time, she'd managed to endear herself to the ED staff. Even patients who showed up repeatedly, using the ED as a primary care office, could win the hearts of the nurses, if they were appreciative of the care and tried to be compliant with the regimen prescribed them.

She turned and lumbered down the hallway behind Lizzy, who lumbered in front of her.

Gary then heard the sound of an ambulance as it pulled up, and then the reverse horn as it was backing into the bay. He watched the video screen as the gurney was pulled out of the rig, and then the medics marched in with the man on the stretcher.

A thin, handsome young man lay on the stretcher bed, his head propped up. He looked disgusted.

The medics turned to Phillips. "What bed, doc?"

"Looks like they're putting you in four. No respiratory problems since the Narcan?"

"No. Just disenchantment."

The weary physician looked at the medic, allowing a hint of amusement to cross his face. What he meant was that the patient, now fully awake, was unhappy and abusive. He watched the stretcher disappear inside the door, with Joanne just behind, ready to triage the patient and gather the report from the medics.

"This doesn't look too impressive to me," he grumbled to Karen, who by this time looked like she'd rather be at home in bed.

"None of these drug OD's look impressive to me, doc, unless they're not breathing when they roll in," came her cynical retort.

Most of the staff had become callous towards patients who indulged in self-abuse, then were carried into the ER, only to repeat the cycle again and again.

"I think I'll go lance that armpit boil. Anything to avoid crossing paths with an angry heroin addict."

"Even Lisa?"

"Yes. Even Lisa."

Lizzy wandered by, and handed the chart to Gary.

"She really needs a bath Dr. Phillips."

"I know, I know, but she is an awfully nice person. And she's crazy about *you* Lizzy."

"That's no excuse for poor hygiene," Lizzy returned, scowling.

Lizzy still wore her nursing pin, earned so proudly fifty years before at a local Catholic nursing school, which had long since closed. The order of her world was seriously threatened by ungrateful patients, unwashed bodies and disrespectful colleagues.

"I'm sure you're right, Lizzy. Could you set me up a tray with a number 11 blade? I'll get some local anesthetic. She is going to yell really loud when I numb her, you know. Be prepared."

"She makes a good deal more noise than she needs to," the nurse sniffed.

"By the way, where are the psych people for this detox fellow? And that fellow who was brought in by his brother?"

"They're in seeing the depressed guy now. It took them a while to get the coverage up on the floor."

One of the medics came over to the desk, sleepy-eyed and moving very slowly. Phillips gave him a weary nod. The typically enthusiastic pre-hospital attendant appeared to be as tired as the physician was. His normally bright brown eyes were reddened and had lost their luster.

"Can I get some coffee?" he asked.

"Come," offered Karen. "It's not fresh, but it has caffeine."

"That'll do," he answered, with satisfaction, and followed her into the grimy little kitchen.

Gary joined their conversation. "Is our heroin addict ready to go yet?"

So often, the drug abusers insisted on leaving as soon as they were awakened, and would then sign out against medical advice. That suited him just fine, as there was little to be gained by counseling them or setting up detox or rehab, unless the patient really wanted it.

"Actually, doc, this guy has become much more reasonable," came the medic's reply. "Not your typical heroin user. I think he'll be willing to cooperate with you and let you look him over."

"That's a switch," Gary said. At this stage of the night, he was perfectly content to let self-abusive players sign out and go back to wherever they'd come from. Maybe this guy had a real health issue to tend to, he reasoned.

The phone rang. Karen called him to talk to the GI consultant for the man with pancreatitis.

"No? Somehow I didn't think so. OK, I'll call him back," Gary found himself apologizing. As he'd predicted, the GI physician did not want to admit the man onto his service, but rather wanted to act as a consultant, with the patient admitted to the primary care provider's service. This would involve far less work on his part. Uninsured patients sometimes became hot potatoes through no fault of their own.

After drawing up the lidocaine to numb the skin of Lisa's axilla, Gary marched into her room. She was more than a little upset at the sight of the needle and syringe.

"Lisa, we go through this every time you come in here for your boils," he pleaded. "We can't open them without numbing the skin over top of the boil."

"It hurts," she said, so loudly that Gary himself was startled, despite his expectations. Lisa never failed to express herself.

He injected the lidocaine while she rolled about in pain, barely able to stay on the bed.

"That will help," he said to her, attempting to calm her down.

"It doesn't help! It doesn't help! Why don't you knock me out?" she cried.

"Lisa, you came here asking for me to do this. Be realistic-I can't do general anesthesia on you because you have an abscess. If you want it cut open under anesthesia I can give you antibiotics and pain medication and refer you to a surgeon. There's still a good chance he'll do it in his office under local, just like we do it here. Now do you want me to do this?" Despite himself, his tone had become irritable and cross.

She was suddenly cowed by his voice.

"Well, yes. But be gentle, doctor."

"I'm always gentle. You know that. But I have to open the abscess and clean it out or it won't heal."

"I know that, doctor, that's why I'm here."

"Just two hours later, and I could've signed this out to Terry, as his first patient for the morning," he thought, wistfully. Lisa always seemed to meander in when Gary was on duty. "Just lucky, I guess."

He prepped the axilla, hoping to improve its odor with the iodine solution. A small amount of pus had drizzled out of the sinus tract which connected the abscess to the skin, and it was indeed quite foul-smelling, he noted.

"This poor woman," he thought. The skin of her axilla was scarred and pockmarked from innumerable abscesses and drainage procedures that had been performed. He wondered if it was her skin flora, or her sweat glands, or poor hygiene that put her at risk for this terrible occurrence again and again.

Working quickly, he incised the skin on top of the abscess, and enlarged the hole. Her eyes widened, and her mouth opened as if to scream. She sucked in her breath, then put her hand over her mouth. The scream was muffled but still fairly loud. She managed to hold completely still for the procedure, which was a feat in itself.

He probed the cavity with a pair of hemostats, and felt the fibrous septations inside, breaking up the separations between the small chambers.

"I'm just opening up the tissue inside so it doesn't come right back, Lisa."

There were tears in her eyes, and she was still holding her mouth.

"I'll have the nurse give you some pain medicine-take a dose as soon as you get home."

He stuffed some gauze packing into the hole, distending it.

"Ouch. I thought you were done," she complained.

"Lisa, I am done. I'm truly sorry to hurt you like that. Our numbing didn't do much, I'm afraid. It's hard to numb the skin over an abscess. Next time, let's get you some medicine for pain and sedation before we start."

"I can't have any pain medicine till I get home," she announced. "I have to catch the 51C in just a few minutes. I can't take any pain medicine till I ride the bus back home."

Gary put his hand on her shoulder.

"We've been through this so many times. I think you could take a pain pill even before you get on the bus. But it's up to you-we'll send you home with a few. And I want you to take antibiotics for a week, since the infection looked like it spread to the skin around your abscess. We call that cellulitis."

"When do I come back?"

"Come back in two days and we'll get that packing out, OK?"

She looked confused.

"What if the hospital's not here in two days?"

"What?"

"My brother told me that they are going to close down the

South Side hospital."

"Lisa, how would he know that?" The physician was growing more and more frustrated at the mere mention of the topic.

"I guess," she surmised, ignoring his reaction, "I could go across the river to Mercy Hospital. Besides, I have a wedding to go to in two days. My cousin is getting married. The wedding is at two o'clock and we're invited. Should I come back to the emergency room before the wedding starts, or after it's over?"

"Lisa," he began, his aggravation giving way to the bemusement he often felt when he worked with Lisa, "you choose. Either one is fine with me. As long as you get the packing out, allright?"

He wasn't going to ask why she would be attending a wedding on a weekday-he was sure the answer would be much too long and convoluted.

Her brow was furrowed as she worked through the possibilities.

"Are you sure it doesn't matter? Because I can come before the wedding or after the wedding. I don't think my cousin will mind if I'm a little late."

"Really, either way is going to work out OK for us." He hastily left the room, as he'd been in these conversations with Lisa before.

She was still talking loudly about her quandary when Lizzy re-entered the room to give her the discharge instructions and her medications.

Gary remarked to himself that Lizzy certainly had a way with words, as listened to her providing instructions. She usually added some wisdom of her own, based on her accumulated years of nursing experience.

"And you know, Lisa," he overheard her saying, "it's really important to bathe yourself frequently. With vigorous scrubbing, with soap and water, we might be able to avoid these infections in the future."

"That's really a good idea, nurse. I'll try to do that. I have a wedding to go to in two days. My cousin is getting married. But I have to come back to the emergency room that day..."

"Cheer up, doc. It's going on five o'clock. Next thing you know, you'll get that morning rush of adrenaline." Karen said sympathetically, as Gary paced by on his way to see the man in bed two.

"The only rush I want is the rush to my bed," he growled. "By the way, did psych come down and see the depressed guy?"

"Yes, doctor, remember I told you he was in seeing the man who wants detox? It's Ronald. He's always a little slower than the others."

"Oh, yeah, definitely slower. But he's very helpful. I'm glad it's him. And who else has the patience to deal with the placement issues?"

The phone rang twice in rapid succession. Gary shook his head. It could only be medic command. He picked up the phone.

"South Side. ED. Phillips."

"Good morning, doc. It's Tim at medic command. I got medic five bound for you with a 78 year old female complaining of shortness of breath. She's got a history of a bypass, hypertension, prior heart failure, hypothyroid, and a stroke. She woke up an hour ago and couldn't breathe. Her BP is 200/110, heart rate is 108 in sinus tachycardia, oxygen saturation 92% on high flow mask O2. She's got rales and wheezes all over both lung fields. She is alert and oriented times three, but very anxious. The medics have started an IV and O2 and they gave her three sprays of sublingual nitro. They report she's somewhat improved but still tachypneic and working to breathe. They'll be at your door in six minutes."

"Very good," he commented, hanging up the receiver.

Ever since his emergency medicine rotation in medical school he'd learned to respect "six-o'clock-CHF." Somehow, early morning seemed to take its toll on many people with congestive heart failure. A patient struggling to breathe, with fluid filling his or her lungs, seemed to show up at that hour virtually every morning in a busy urban ER.

"Lizzy," he called. "It sounds like pulmonary edema."

She nodded, also not surprised. "I'll get an intubation tray ready."

"And make up a nitrogycerine drip," he requested.

He decided to visit the man who'd overdosed on heroin before the new patient arrived in the ambulance. Entering the exam room, Gary found a well-groomed, polite man sitting on the stretcher in no distress. He smiled at the physician in a very congenial way. His face had a very youthful appearance; his blue eyes showed a bit of uncertainty. Not just uncertainty about his surroundings or circumstances, Gary thought, but uncertainty about his life in general.

"You went on a heroin binge?" the doctor asked, matter-of-factly.

"Well, yes... I've been using for a few months. But nothing

like this. Today, I don't even know what happened. I shot up, and next thing I know, the medics are bringing me here. I wasn't trying to die. I guess I just used too much at once."

"Yeah, I understand. The quality control out there isn't so good. Maybe it was much more potent than you realized. What can I do for you now?"

Gary looked steadily into the man's eyes.

"I don't know. I don't think I'm sick. But I don't ever want to end up like this again."

"Are you depressed?"

"Right now, yes."

"Have you been having any thoughts of harming yourself or others?"

"No. At least I don't think so."

Gary heaved a sigh of relief. A little social service help or a visit from the psych service while he was in the ER, to set up some outpatient counseling would set this man straight, without the song and dance of a psych transfer or admission. At least he wouldn't have to fight with an obstinate psychiatrist to get him admitted.

"Well, let me examine you, you know, from a medical standpoint, and that. After that, I'll have someone from the psychiatry floor come down and talk to you, and he can help us work on some counseling, probably as an outpatient. OK? But please be patient. I've got kind of a backup of problems for the psychiatry people to handle tonight."

"I really do need help, doc. Whatever you can do for me, I appreciate it. Something has to change. I can't keep living life this way."

His eyes began to glisten as he related his situation, and the reluctant physician tried to comfort him, putting his hand on the forlorn man's shoulder.

"I know you can't. We'll work on getting you into therapy- to try to break this cycle you're in."

Retiring to his desk, he contemplated the situation. He was aware that the patient might be telling a half-truth. And the weary emergency physician was truly interested in getting the man some help. But it was incredibly frustrating to make it happen. After the "medical clearance" was established, which might or might not require drug testing to substantiate the obvious, the rusty, inefficient engine of the mental health system would swing into action. The psych tech would come see him; usually agreeing that he needed help. But the tech was himself a marionette dancing on

131

the strings of an insurance system that allowed little and denied much. Only when patients were sick enough to require hospitalization, by virtue of suicidal ideation or frank psychosis, could he steer them directly into the medico-psychiatric system. But falling short of this, as most psych complaints did, he handed them off to a patchwork, underfunded outpatient system that really seemed to do very little for them. Too often, Gary or one of his colleagues would see them come back, more beaten down by their bad choices in life, sometimes beyond meaningful intervention.

His reverie was suddenly interrupted.

"Doctor, what's happening with my wife?"

He looked up, startled, to see the impatient husband of the woman in bed five, whose suffering had been little changed by his interventions.

"Sir, I'm waiting to find out about the CT scan we just sent her for."

"Can she have some water?"

"I'd rather she didn't, in case she has an abscess or something that needs surgery tonight."

The man's eyes widened in surprise. "Surgery? Tonight?"

"Sorry, I didn't mean to alarm you. It's at least a possibility. I just want to see the scan results before she puts anything in her stomach."

The man was becoming increasingly frustrated by the wait. And both he and his wife were getting impatient in the face of multiple negative tests: the normal UA, the normal chest X-ray. This aspect of emergency medicine was terribly unsatisfying for him. Often, there was no time to sit and talk with patients, no time to explain fully what was happen, or to nurture them or show that he cared.

"I should have an answer within a couple of minutes for you, sir," Gary said, apologetically. "I'll let you know as soon as I get called."

Fortuitously, the phone rang at that moment.

"Doc, it's Dr. John for you again," Karen called with mock cheerfulness.

He frowned as he walked to the phone, preparing for a battle of wits.

"No Bill, as I predicted, the GI guys won't admit this man primarily, they'll only see him in consultation. But look, this guy needs to be admitted..."

Karen squinted at him, studying that various expressions

that played across his countenance as he spoke to his uncooperative colleague.

"Bill, you're on call. This is your responsibility. I will not transfer him to the University Clinic Service. That's called dumping, and we could all get nailed by the Feds-you, me and the hospital. No way. I will write your orders and get him admitted. Tomorrow, you'll round on him, or find someone to do it for you."

Again, the physician at the other end of the line protested.

"Then I will phone the administrator on-call, and the chief of the medical staff RIGHT NOW!"

He was shouting, and suddenly, looking around, felt all eyes on him. He became quiet as he hung up the phone.

"I should not have to go through this," he said quietly.

"Just write the orders, doc. He'll be in to round on the man. You got the best of him that time, " Karen offered, handing him a blank order sheet.

5a.m.

Lizzy's voice echoed down the hallway. "Doc, the medics are here. Can you come to room three, please."

He moved quickly from one bedside to the next. He was truly exhausted, and the night began to seem surreal to him, as though he was watching someone else go through the motions in *his* body.

"Another two hours," he thought, glancing at the clock, "and I can get out of here."

"We found her sitting up on her bed, pale and soaking wet, diaphoretic as can be," said the breathless paramedic. Gary knew him well. Murphy was young and excitable, but reliable and possessed of sound judgement. He was on the heavy side, and when he got excited, his face became very ruddy.

"When I listened to her, she sounded really wet. She could barely speak but told us she had a history of bypass and heart failure. She's been admitted a few times for what sounds like pulmonary edema. The first oxygen saturation was 82% on room air and it went up to 90% on high flow oxygen. Her pressure was up, and so was her heart rate. We started mask O2, and got orders from medic command for lasix 40 milligrams IV. Then, we gave her nitrospray sublingual times six en route. She's a little better, but her oxygen saturations are still in the low 90's, even on the high flow oxygen."

The paramedic reported his findings as though he were an

133

automaton, intent on justifying his actions and making his motivation clear. The physician could see that he'd been well-trained, and that his ability to apply his knowledge to the situation at hand meant a lot to him. He nodded, thanking the medic for his report, and turned to the patient.

"Ma'am, you've had fluid on your lungs before? From heart failure?"

She nodded, her pale skin glistening with a light coating of perspiration.

"Did the medicine under your tongue help you?" he asked, pressing his stethoscope against her clammy white skin.

"I think so," she gasped.

"It sounds very wet," he said. "Let's keep trying to get that fluid off."

"Lizzy, can you push another 60 milligrams of lasix for us? And start a nitroglycerine drip at ten micrograms per minute? What do you have for the blood pressure?"

"We're getting it now-there: 190/100."

"Let's get an EKG, and the usual cardiac labs, chest X-ray and old records. Have Karen call for respiratory, and ask them to bring the BiPAP," he said, requesting the noninvasive ventilator.

All through his residency and the first ten years of his practice, respiratory failure had foreshadowed a host of undesirable interventions and consequences: insertion of an endotracheal tube followed by mechanical ventilation. Sedation. Paralysis. Cardiovascular instability. Airway trauma. Iatrogenic infections. Often, it was the initiation of a series of seemingly inevitable complications that led to multiple organ system failure, and, eventually, death. But noninvasive ventilation with a face mask, in certain patients, had allowed physicians to turn away from that pathway. It just seemed as though there was less injury to the patient, less trauma to a collapsing physiology. Studies had born it out, in selected patients: improved outcome, better cost-effectiveness, less time in the ICU. This lady seemed a very good candidate.

He turned back to the patient.

"When you came in the hospital for heart failure last year, were you on a breathing machine?"

Her eyes widened. "Please don't put that tube down my throat!" she gasped.

"We don't do that unless we need to as a lifesaving measure-but sometimes we have to. Do you understand?"

She looked at him fearfully, neither agreeing nor refusing.

134

"I don't think your lungs are going to be able to continue working this hard. You're going to need some assistance. We can try something a little bit less hard on you that still helps you breathe-it's a mask with pressurized oxygen in it to help you take easier breaths. Let's give it a try."

Wiping a stinging, oily sweat from his eyes, Gary stepped back and looked at her, doubtfully. She appeared to be fatiguing. She was tight and wet, and she'd been working hard for a while, probably for hours. BiPAP might not be sufficient to keep her off the ventilator.

"Eddie, welcome back," he said to the therapist as he appeared.

"I need an albuterol treatment and a blood gas. She's mostly wet, but she's wheezing as well. Right after the nebulized treatment, or even at the same time, I want to start her on BiPAP. Let's start with pressures of 12 inspiratory and 8 expiratory, OK?"

The handsome, olive-skinned therapist nodded and began to set up the BiPAP. The physician felt a bit helpless as the nurses and respiratory tech set about carrying out his orders. He watched on anxiously, impressed with the energy and intent. This was about all he could offer: oxygen, nitroglycerine, diuresis to remove fluid, noninvasive ventilation, perhaps a little morphine to calm the patient. There wasn't much else to do except wait and pray. The lady looked a little out of it already, he thought. Morphine might really knock her out. Still, she was anxious and her eyes were wide and frightened as she struggled to breath.

"Maryanne," he said, addressing the other nurse, who had come in to help out. "Can you get us two milligrams of IV morphine as well? Let's see if we can take the edge off her anxiety without sedating too much."

"OK, doctor."

As if I didn't already give you enough to do, he thought. He held the old lady's hand while a second IV was started on the other side. She was moist and cool in her extremities, a very bad combination. He looked at her mouth and neck, assessing whether it would be difficult to see her larynx with a laryngoscope if he needed to put in an endotracheal tube. The chin was a little recessed, and her neck was short and thick. It seemed to have a normal range of motion. Her mouth was small, and she had a full set of teeth. She could be a bit of a challenge, he decided. Hopefully, I won't have to find out.

"Dr. Phillips-what FIO2 do you want to start with? 90 per cent?"

135

"Yes, Eddie, 90 per cent sounds fine for now. Let just try to keep her oxygen saturations above 92 per cent if we can. If we can wean it down, so much the better."

"I'll be back shortly with the blood gas," the respiratory technician replied, walking briskly past the nurses desk and towards his STAT lab.

Gary admired Eddie. He was dutiful, kind to patients, and competent. "Give me an army of men like Eddie, he thought, and I could really get things done."

He set up the BiPAP machine, applying the mask tightly to the patient's face. She looked distressed by the mask, as most patients did. But within a few breaths, she managed to synchronize her breathing with the machine. It made a curious hissing sound, pressurizing the inhaled gas. He could see her straining less, her diaphoresis slowly disappearing. The noise and effort of her breathing seemed lessened almost immediately. Her face appeared decidedly calmer, and she slowly reclined against the raised back of the stretcher.

"Well, that seems to be working, anyway," he mumbled to Maryann.

"Yes, she does look better, doctor."

Eddie appeared again. "Here's that gas, doctor Phillips."

"Hmmm. She's acidemic. The pCO_2 is up to 67. Looks pretty ugly. With these numbers, I think she was clearly going to fail, and soon. But clinically, Eli, she's turned the corner. Let's sit on this for a while. The diuretic is probably starting to work. Do we have a Foley catheter in?"

"Now that she's more settled, we can work on that," Joanne replied.

Gary rubbed his red eyes, and asked "Is psych here yet?"

"Yes, doctor." She grinned, amused at the physician's forgetfulness at this hour. "Randall is in with the first guy now."

"Oh, great." He sat down and felt the weight of the long night descend on him.

"Did you let him know about our heroin-abusing friend who wants detox?"

"Yes, doctor, he decided to see that other man first because of his depression."

Again the phone rang. It was the radiologist, who had found nothing in the abdominal CT of the lady in five. "Great," Gary thought. "Fever, abdominal pain, nausea, flank pain, a recent UTI, a headache, loss of appetite, a tender belly and flanks. What the hell is wrong with this lady?"

He walked into her room and sat down. Looking at both the wary patient and the expectant husband, he explained his reasoning.

"I can't find anything. It could be just a virus."

Patients hated to hear that, as if it wasn't really an illness at all.

"It's highly unlikely, but with fever and a headache, we should exclude meningitis."

The patient looked at him intently, expecting the worst.

"That means a lumbar puncture-you know, a spinal tap. There's no other test to make this diagnosis, or exclude it."

She looked resigned. Her husband looked concerned, even fearful. The term "spinal tap" seemed to carry a bevy of unrealistic fears with it. He tried to allay their anxiety. Then, approaching the desk, he asked Karen to stamp a consent form and Lizzy to set up an LP tray with some extra local anesthetic.

At the nurse's station, he sat and pored over the EKG from the lady with pulmonary edema. Gary felt his eyes glaze over and begin to close. A hazy sleep enveloped him and his head began to bob. It was a pleasant sensation, and he hadn't any desire to interfere with it.

"Doctor ?" His eyes snapped open.

"Sorry to bother you. I just wanted to talk to you about this patient." It was Randall, the psychiatric technician. Soft spoken, caring, a true patient advocate. He just wasn't very speedy.

"Well, he is depressed, and has expressed suicidal ideation. And clearly he has a drug dependency problem. With the dual-diagnosis we can admit him here. If the psychiatrist on-call will accept him."

"OK, fine with me. If not, we go over to Western Psych, right?"

"I think they would take him. That's his catchment area, anyway. Problem is, he doesn't want to go there. Apparently he went there once in the past and it wasn't conducive to his psychological well-being. He hated it."

"Are there alternatives?"

"Yes, St. Francis is one. I'll explore that next, if need be. He's willing to sign in. But if we have to send him to Western Psych, then we have to commit him involuntarily."

"I can do that, but I'd rather not since he's actively seeking help on his own."

"I understand, doctor. It'd be a real hassle, compared to the voluntary commitment."

"I'll say," Gary replied.

Calling the county to request the commitment and filling out all their papers was frustrating enough. Getting called to go to court for the commitment hearing in two or three days was much worse.

A glint of gray morning light began to filter into the department through the glass ambulance doors. The exhausted doctor felt a wave of wakeful energy course through him, and the bleak depression of the wee hours began to ebb away.

He could see the old lady in room three, gesturing to Joann about something or other that she wanted. She no longer looked like she would die, at least not then and there. As expected, her chest X-ray showed that the lungs were full of fluid. In particular, "pulmonary edema" meant that the air spaces in the lung had been flooded with fluid that had been forced, under pressure, from the blood vessels that surrounded them. She was literally drowning in her own vital fluids. The BiPAP machine, however, which could be heard hissing as it assisted each of her inhalations, had bought her enough time to start redistributing and urinating out the extra volume. Her long-term prognosis was pretty poor, but she'd live to see another day.

The blood had arrived for the man with the GI bleeding. Gary had heard loud gagging as the nurse apparently had introduced the nasogastric tube, to exclude the stomach as the source of the bleeding. Gary walked in to check on him and his wife.

"How are you, sir?"

"A little cold. I think it's from the blood. I'm just glad to have that tube out of my nose."

"I bet," the physician agreed. "Nobody likes the NG tube. Luckily for me, the nurses have to put them in. I don't get blamed, even though I'm the one who orders it."

"I'll remember that," the patient said, chuckling, "for next time."

His blood pressure was now normal, and a hint of ruddiness had crept into his white cheeks as the blood was infused.

"I'll give Dr. Taylor a call, and we'll get you a bed upstairs," Gary explained.

The man nodded and smiled, apparently grateful for the modicum of attention that the busy doctor could afford him. He then made the familiar trek to the secretary's desk, looking at test results that had been laid there for his evaluation.

"Karen, the enzymes on that lady in two are normal, the

EKG is basically unchanged-let's call her attending and get her an ICU bed. He may be in the house on rounds by now. I've got the old records, and I'll start writing orders now."

Her attending, an internist named Harrison, called back a few seconds later.

He was all business, and quite awake at that hour. "That sounds good, put her on lasix IV twice a day and keep her on the nitro drip. We'll start her on a milrinone infusion in the ICU. Set up an echo-she hasn't had one in a couple years."

"I will. I'm looking at the results of the last one. She had preserved systolic function, and diastolic dysfunction."

The heart's muscular contractions were strong, and the amount of blood pumped with each contraction was virtually normal. However, the heart muscle was abnormally stiff, predisposing to a high back-pressure that overwhelmed the lungs capillaries, allowing fluid to spill out of the vessels and into the lungs themselves. One solution was to reduce the load against which the ventricles had to pump, by dilating the systemic arterial vessels.

"Fine. We'll up her vasodilators after she gets out of the ICU," answered the attending. "Thanks very much. See you later."

Gary hung up. "Boy, he talks fast. He has an incredible knowledge of his patients, though."

The rotund secretary laughed. "Most of the time, I can't even understand him, I have to say, doc."

She looked sleepily around at the ED. The nurses were still moving quickly from patient to patient, but there was a sense that all the patients had been seen, and things were under control.

"Looks like we kept the citizens of Southside safe for another night."

"Well, I wish it was over," Gary replied, gloomily. He didn't have the energy for many more encounters.

"Now, I need to do that LP for the lady in five. Did Lizzy get the kit out for me?" He craned his neck and could see the tray and other paraphernalia on a table in the room.

"Lizzy," he called out, not willing to look around for her. "I think I'll need some sedation, too. Can you get two milligrams of midazolam and 100 micrograms of fentanyl? That should do it. I'll get the consent."

He went to the bedside of the febrile lady, who had finally begun to look as though she were responding to his therapy. She lay, with apparent comfort, on the cart, with a blanket doubled up beneath her head.

139

"Mrs. Hammersmith, I'll go ahead and do the spinal tap now. I need to get your consent for the procedure, first."

"Consent?" she asked, smiling as best she could manage. She did actually look brighter and less distressed, he thought.

"Consent to put a big needle in my spine? Sounds wonderful! Sure, where do I sign?"

Despite his pessimistic outlook at that hour, Gary had to grin. Clearly she did feel better, if she could manage a little sarcasm. If she'd been this jovial all night, he'd never even have thought about tapping her. It was too late now, the decision was made, and he'd stick to it. Despite the fever and headache, his instincts told him that this patient did not have meningitis. Still, with no other explanation, it was time to "rule out" the possibility.

Her husband rose reluctantly from his chair. "I'm taking off for now, doc. I can't hang around for this kind of thing. Please, take good care of her."

"I will," the physician said, regarding the man with a serious expression.

He presented the form for her to sign. She took the pen and placed her signature as he explained the risks.

"Overall, a lumbar puncture is really quite safe. I'll use a small needle to try to reduce any chance of spinal headache."

"Good," she replied, with a hint of humor in her voice. "I don't think I could bear another one on top of this one."

Gary frowned as he examined her bare back. She was ample, with rolls of round flesh about her middle. As she lay on her side, the adipose layers hung downward towards the floor. Even her back was chubby. He couldn't palpate the spine at all. He felt for her iliac crests, imagined the midline, and inserted the local anesthetic with the long needle that he liked to use to find his way. It went in without any problem, but he wasn't sure he was even down to the spinous processes of the backbone, yet, let alone the ligaments that protected the passageway to the nerve roots and their protective sac.

"OK, now you may feel pressure," he pointed out. The nurse had already given the patient the sedation he'd asked for, and she was very comfortable. He heard her begin to snore.

"Lizzy, keep an eye on her oxygen saturation, would you? It didn't take much to sedate her-she's a pretty cheap date, it seems."

"She's fine, doctor-98% on her oxygen."

Then, he found the boney resistance of her spinous process. She stiffened and groaned, but didn't awaken. He angled towards

140

her upper back, and the needle slid between the processes. He felt the satisfying "pop" of the dura mater as the needle tented the tough tissue and impaled it. He removed the stylet from the needle.

"Ahh, the CSF is crystal clear. I bet there won't be a single red or white cell. 'Champagne' we used to call it, when I was in my rotations over at Children's Hospital."

Lizzy raised her eyebrows, and apparently was not impressed with his accomplishment.

"Just write your orders for the testing, Dr. Phillips. I'll get the tubes to Karen to label and send to the lab. Make sure it's really clear which tube is supposed to go for what test. I think Maryann just brought in a couple more patients for you to see."

"Oh, well" he mumbled, looking anxiously at the clock.

6a.m.

Gary reported to his desk again, sitting beside the secretary, who had briefly dozed off. She shook her head and looked towards him.

"Doc, I put your labs on your desk."

He looked at the scattered papers, trying to figure out what belonged to which patient. He found the urinalysis of the man with pain on urination. It was normal. "Well," he thought, "I can tell him it's normal and send him off to his urologist later this week. Or, I can try to convince him that I need to do a rectal exam and check his prostate. Pretty unlikely cause of his symptoms, but with the language barrier, I can't trust the history. God knows what he'd tell me if his English was better."

The little, round African man had been sitting for two hours, waiting patiently on his bed with his head in his hands. He looked up hopefully at the physician, but his face fell when he saw the physician reach for latex gloves and lubricant. This was a clear indication of an impending rectal exam, in any language.

"No... infection?" he asked uncertainly.

"No sir. I'm afraid I'll have to check your prostate."

"Prostate?"

"Yes, sir. Can you drop your pants and bend forward over the bed, like this?" Gary gestured for the man.

Now the dark-skinned man looked genuinely startled. He held up his hands with the palms open as a mild sign of protest. The physician was in no mood to negotiate. He forced the issue.

"Just bend over and drop your pants, it's a little
141

uncomfortable, but not painful."

"But..." the man implored.

"You're in luck. Look how small my fingers are. If Dr. Schultze, my partner, was here, this would be a lot more unpleasant."

Grumbling softly, the patient bent forward with his pants lowered. He seemed to be speaking his mother tongue as he lowered his head.

"Now, relax your buttocks...if you tighten up, I can't do this..."

"Ohhh, no, doctor," he continued to protest, even as he complied.

"Try to relax-there. Now does that hurt?"

Gary pushed his finger against the prostate gland, which was sizable and a little boggy. His fingers weren't particularly large, but they could usually reach their target. There were no palpable nodules in the gland.

The man struggled to move forward but had no room to move.

"Yes, doctor," he said. "Pain."

"Hmmm..." said the physician, removing his finger. "The prostate is enlarged, and boggy. I think the gland is infected. The short course of antibiotics you were on probably didn't cover it. Let's get you on something with better prostate penetration, for a longer duration. I'll call the urologist to let him know. I better check the stool for blood, too, while we're here."

He smeared some brown residue on the hemoccult card, and placed a drop of developer onto it.

"No. It looks okay. Nothing to worry about there."

The man looked a little hurt.

"Sir, I didn't mean to cause you pain. That area is always a little tender. But if it's infected, it's very sore, and yours really was. I'll write you a prescription and get your first dose of antibiotics here in the ER. You don't have to wait till I talk to the urologist. I'll just let him know."

At that, the patient seemed pleased, and Gary was a bit relieved. He had definitely bent the man to his will, but he felt it was necessary, and helpful. Paternalism wasn't his usual way of practicing medicine, but at times, he found it a most helpful philosophy.

"Doctor Phillips, it's medic command," Karen's voice called him on the overhead.

"Again? They're trying to keep us busy, I guess," he said,

142

dejectedly, walking to the phone at the nursing station.

"Doctor, medic two is on the way in with an elderly female- 82 years old- with shortness of breath and lightheadedness. Her initial blood pressure was 85 over 50 and her heart rate was 110. She was treated with 500 cc's of normal saline and her pressure is up to 100 over 60. Her oxygen saturation is 99% on high flow O2. They have established an IV and should see you in about 15 minutes. She is a little confused, with clear lungs and dry skin. She is oriented to place and person. Any further orders?"

He thought about the presentation for a moment.

"Does she have any medical history?"

"Just high blood pressure," the man replied.

"Can they send me an EKG?"

"I"ll ask them to do that. They sent one to us at command, and it just shows sinus tachycardia."

"Fine. Tell them to keep the fluids going. I'll see her when they get here," he said, his voice a bit hoarse from talking most of the night.

"As if I would say anything else," he thought.

He looked up at the box, which contained a lone chart. Hoping to see the patient and start the workup before the medics arrived, he picked it up. Making his way to the back of the ED, he found in room eight a delightful, spirited woman named Stella who had fallen the prior evening. When her arm pain would not subside, she called her daughter, who dutifully brought her to the ED. At 91 years of age, she still lived alone in her own small row house, three blocks from the hospital. The woman had tried to break her fall as she lost her balance, but her brittle limbs had failed her and she now could not move her right arm at the shoulder.

Gary was all too familiar with Stella, even though he'd never met her before. She was an archetype on the South Side: a stooped, plump little Polish (or Czech, or Slovak, or Ukrainian,) lady, an immigrant herself, or the first-generation offspring of an immigrant steelworker. Such women were often widowed at this stage of their lives, having spent five or six decades taking care of a mill-worker husband and their children. Strolling up and down the streets of the Southside flats or the steep, twisting avenues of the slopes, one would encounter these little ladies everywhere, pulling their spindly two-wheeled wire grocery carts to market, shoveling snow from their sidewalks and porches, cleaning the front windows of their diminutive row homes. For most of them, life had been difficult, but they bore their burdens with a spirit of devotion and pride. Ceaseless, tireless effort defined their generation. Now, bereft of their mates, few of them could conceive of living outside of their homes, and many labored steadfastly on, keeping house for no one, asserting an independence that was necessary for existence. Gary saw his own Polish grandmother in each of them: hardworking, unyielding, staunchly Catholic (or orthodox), usually kind, but at times remarkably close-minded. His Grandmother's own struggle had finally come to a close just a year before, after 18 months of illness and psychological deterioration. He felt an enormous respect for these women, was honored to care for them.

"Do you think it's broken, doctor?" she asked, smiling bravely despite the pain she was in. It was a happy surprise, and fairly unusual, to meet someone of her age who was still so clearly in control of her faculties.

The physician pushed gingerly over the proximal humerus, noting the swelling and bruising, which was expanding even has he examined her.

"Can you squeeze my hand? Can you flex and extend the fingers? Move your thumb like this..." He gestured, testing the innervation to the muscles of her hand and forearm.

She did as he asked, splinting her arm to her side to avoid any motion of the shoulder. The distal nerve function was intact, and her pulses were normal.

"There's a pretty good chance she's fractured it," he explained to the patient and her family.

He was softening the blow. Surely, he figured, she'd fractured it. He put is arms out in front of him and feigned to fall forward, demonstrating the fracture mechanism.

"This is a common injury in older folks when they fall onto outstretched arms."

The aged woman looked down, sullen. This would certainly be a challenge to her independence. The physician could sense from the family's dynamics that her ability to live by herself had already been under question. Now, she'd fallen and injured herself, perhaps seriously. She'd be relegated to the use of one hand and arm for weeks, perhaps months.

"I'll order some X-rays. Do you need any medication for pain?"

"No," she answered sternly. "If I don't move it, it doesn't hurt that much."

Her daughter coaxed her, "Mother, it has to hurt. Take a pain pill, already, and try to get the pain under control."

144

"I don't need it," the lady fussed back.

"If it is fractured, I'll call your doctor for a referral to an orthopedist. They don't usually operate on this type of injury, unless it's very severe. We'll put your shoulder in an immobilizer until the follow-up appointment."

He turned to exit, and heard the mother and daughter begin to hash out the details of her new existence in the daughter's house. It sounded like a petty argument, Gary thought, but what it really meant was that this young woman would not think of abandoning her mother to a nursing facility when she herself could offer her help. It was Pittsburgh through and through. Gritty, unglamorous and sincere.

He wandered out to find Russell discussing the case of Bartholomew with the restless brother.

"Mr. Razkosky," the soft-spoken tech explained, with just a hint of authority, "I don't usually perform these kinds of services out of the emergency department. It's very unusual for someone who'd just been released from weeks of psychiatric hospitalization to show up in another hospital's ER on the very same day of discharge, hoping to accomplish the long-term placement on the spot. It simply isn't done this way."

Then, his voice fell to its usual soft, amicable tone. He apparently felt he'd been stern enough.

"But I've made a few phone calls tonight, and I think I've found a place that your brother can go. We'll arrange transport after breakfast. It's about 15 minutes from here, so you and your mother should be able to visit your brother whenever you'd like to."

Gary watched on, pleased that Randall was able to accommodate this man and his brother, without another psychiatric hospitalization. Karen's voice, which had become rather husky in the early morning, interrupted the emergency physician's reverie.

"Doc, the medics are here."

He picked up his tempo as he saw how rapidly the medics were bringing the stretcher in from the gray, cool mists of the dawn. "Now what?" he wondered.

"Morning again, Doc. This young lady called because she was weak and short of breath-it started last night. She denies any chest pain or vomiting. She also denies bloody or black stools. We found her sitting back on her couch, cool and diaphoretic. Her initial pulse was 130, her blood pressure only 80 over 40. The oxygen saturations were in the low 90's but her fingers were cold and she wasn't perfusing well, and that. She was alert but a little confused, oriented times two..."

"Is she moving everything?" he asked.

"Yes sir. No neuro deficits. Once we spoke to her and started our IV, she came around. We bolused her with 300 cc's of saline, and her pressure increased to 95 over 60; her heart rate came down to 110. She's sort of slipping back down, now. Her last pressure was about 90 systolic."

Gary turned to the patient. She looked completely enervated, almost devoid of life. Shocky, he thought.

"Ma'am, hello. I'm Doctor Phillips and I work here in the emergency room. Have you had any chest pressure or pain? How is your breathing now? Any leg swelling?"

He needed information first, and he fired his questions at her in quick succession. She was barely up to the task of answering them. Confused and listless as she was, her answers came quite slowly. Her voice was barely audible against the noisy backdrop of the department.

"I, uh, I don't think I'm having any pain. I just feel dizzy and weak..."

"Any abdominal pain? Or headache, or loss of sensation or strength in an arm or leg?"

She looked at him, blankly.

Suddenly, Lizzy looked up from her attempts to obtain vital signs. She always looked stern, but additional concern was apparent in her officious expression.

"Doctor Phillips, I'm not getting a blood pressure."

She stopped cycling the automatic cuff and pulled a manual sphygmomanometer over to the bedside. Again and again she inflated the cuff. Gary put his hand on the patient's wrist and then her groin, but he could detect no pulse. She had become unresponsive, her eyelids descending and her eyes rolling upward. The nurse and physician quickly put the head of the stretcher down to the horizontal, and then tilted the entire bed to a head down position. He felt the neck for a carotid pulse. It was weak and thready, barely palpable. Her systolic blood pressure is probably only 60 or so, he thought.

The physician observed the calmness and pallor of her face. She looked peaceful, as though she was not distressed by the proceedings around her, or by her own situation. He wondered what she was actually experiencing at the moment, whether it was sublime or simply nothingness.

"Lizzy, get me another IV, draw some blood for labs and a

type and crossmatch. I've no idea why she's hypotensive."

As her head moved back, her eyes opened, and she looked around her. The blood pressure now registered 80/40 on the monitor. The IV fluids were infusing as rapidly as the lines permitted, and the group in attendance noticed with some satisfaction that she seemed to be responding. At least she was alert again, and able to breathe comfortably, protecting her own airway.

Gary systematically evaluated her. She was tachycardic and hypotensive, with clear lungs and normal heart sounds. No abnormal heart rhythm, no congestive heart failure, no signs of bleeding or swelling anywhere to account for volume loss that could have caused her low blood pressure. Why, then was her pressure so low, he wondered? That left, among diagnostic possibilities, an extensive myocardial infarction as the number one choice. He also had to consider a pulmonary thromboembolism, a tension pneumothorax, a valvular rupture, bacteremia with septic shock, or a severe allergic reaction. None of these choices looked likely from his exam, but blood clots that moved from the legs to the lung, known as pulmonary emboli. The clots themselves were notoriously difficult to diagnose, and often lay clinically silent until one of them in the legs or in the pelvis broke free, making its way to the right heart and the major lung blood vessels, which they would then obstruct. The right heart would then struggle in the face of this new oppressive loading condition, and often fail, killing the patient in short order.

"I need an EKG and chest film right now. Call Eddie to come run us a blood gas. Let's hang dopamine along with the volume infusions until I can figure out what I'm dealing with."

He was distracted by Karen, who was calling him to the desk.

"Dr. Phillips, it's Dr. John again, on the phone."

He looked at Lizzy.

"Tell him, please, that I can't come to the phone right now. Lizzy, try to get another pressure for me, would you?"

The registration clerk appeared at the door.

"We can't locate any family for her-she lives alone. A neighbor found her and phoned EMS. He's supposed to be on the way. Maybe he has some more information about her."

Gary began to feel a sickening panic. The systolic blood pressure was again only in the 70's, barely enough to perfuse the vascular beds in her heart and brain. Either or both might fail at any moment. The lady's hearth rate remained quite elevated, but she could still talk. She wasn't capable of giving a history, and the medics had not been able to get much from her, either. All Gary knew was that she had a history of low thyroid function, and hypertension. That wasn't much help.

"Get me an intubation tray, too, Lizzy. Where is that X-ray tech?"

The respiratory tech arrived, and began palpating the pulse in the wrist to draw a blood gas specimen.

"Eddie, that's not gonna work. Let me get you a femoral stick. She's just not perfusing well enough to get a blood gas stick at the radial artery."

The physician felt the groin with his fingertips. There was a thready pulse, and he plunged the long needle into the inguinal fold. The patient, who was mumbling incoherently to herself, seemed not to feel this.

"OK, Doctor, here's another IV line..."

Maryann had prepared the dopamine infusion and connected it to the IV cannula she'd inserted. By providing constriction of the vessels, this drug could increase the blood pressure to more acceptable levels, as well as stimulating the heart to pump more effectively. Eventually, he'd have to insert a larger IV into the neck veins to handle the fluids and infusions that a critically ill patient required, but for now, the peripheral IVs would do.

Again, Lizzy listened with her stethoscope for the sounds that indicated the pressure, which now was only 65/30. "I'm losing her," thought the physician. The cold, stark reality of the patient's impending death suddenly touched him. If she progressed to cardiac arrest, he was sure she would die, despite drugs and resuscitation measures. Something this bad, causing decompensation this fast, was probably not survivable in a patient this old.

Maryann handed him the EKG tracing, and he scanned it quickly. "Sinus tachycardia," he thought, "and some nonspecific ST and T wave changes." Certainly this was not a classic myocardial infarction by EKG criteria, and not what he expected.

"I don't have a pulse, doctor," Lizzy called out, sternly.

"OK- Get me an intubation set. I'll start ventilating her with the bag. Open both IV's all the way, and the dopamine wide open, too. Call the attending for me-maybe he can give me a clue about this lady's background. I can let him know what's going on, if we can resuscitate her. Start the chest compressions and give me an amp of epinephrine."

"Get Eddie back down here, Karen," he called out, hoping she could hear him.

The team worked frantically, and the nursing supervisor arrived to help. Gary relinquished the face mask ventilation to the respiratory therapist and assembled his equipment for intubation, testing the light on the laryngoscope. And then, just as he prepared to look into the mouth, and despite the cricoid pressure over the front of the neck that was provided by the nursing supervisor, a yellow, thin vomitus erupted from the patient's mouth and nose, propelled by the chest compressions. The physician grabbed the suction, and quickly began clearing the airway, inserting the laryngoscope. He had an excellent view of the larynx and was readily able to place the endotracheal tube.

"Wonderful," he said between his clenched teeth. "As if she didn't have enough problems. Now she's probably got lungs full of vomit. Let's start the ventilations and chest compressions again. What's the rhythm? It looks like it's still sinus tachycardia."

He felt for the carotid pulsation in the neck as the CPR was briefly interrupted. There was no palpable pulse. The respiratory therapist was now ventilating the patient by hand, utilizing a resuscitation bag attached to the endotracheal tube that Gary had inserted.

"Pulseless electrical activity, right doctor?" noted Maryann, describing the Advanced Cardiac Life Support protocol attached to this sort of arrest. "I think we're doing all the right things."

"Yeah, PEA," repeated Gary, looking hopelessly at the monitor. "I bet it's a big MI or a pulmonary embolus. I guess she could've bled somewhere inside but there's certainly no sign of it on my exam. And I don't think she's septic."

"I have a good pulse with your CPR," he said, placing his fingers on the neck again. He felt a sense of hopelessness as he tried to work his way through the differential diagnosis.

"Let's repeat the epinephrine bolus, and go ahead and hang a drip. We've nothing to lose. Can we get the Doppler to check for any blood flow, to see if we're missing a pulse? Keep the fluids open, and I'll recheck breath sounds. Her neck veins are normal and her lungs are clear. Her belly is soft and flat. Eddie, did you bring the blood gas back?"

"Yes, Doctor Phillips. I was just going to give the slip to you- pH of 7.24, pCO2 is 25, pO2 is 62, and bicarbonate is 16."

"And that was a room air gas?"

"No, sir. That was on oxygen. Just before she arrested."

"Ahhh. So she was very hypoxemic. She's most likely had a
149

big pulmonary embolism."

"What else can we do for her, doctor?" Lizzy asked.

"Probably not much, Liz. We could add a thrombolytic agent. She's dying. We've nothing to lose. Can you mix and hang a bolus of tPA? "

Julie, the nursing supervisor turned and hurriedly went to the medication room to prepare the infusion of the thrombolytic agent, a last-gasp effort to break up the clot and reestablish effective blood flow through the lungs. Gary felt physically sick inside. The lady was clearly going to die. As the sequence of events carried him along, he made decisions in reflexive ways. He lived this horror each time someone died unexpectedly. Thankfully, it happened rarely, but still it shocked and appalled him, filling him with grief. As callous as it seemed to admit it, the death of some patients was inevitable. After four years of medical school and a residency, one became comfortable with the idea that many patients would never leave the hospital, despite the efforts of nurses and doctors. But a patient dying on his watch, in his hands-that was something else again. A personal affront, a sickening tragedy, a terrible, wrenching failure to be avoided at all costs. No man on earth who had not faced this could understand how a physician feels when his patient lay dying in front of him, refractory to all his therapeutic efforts, Gary surmised.

Such were the physician's feelings at this moment. The patient's downward spiral into the dark maelstrom of death would not be interrupted. The woman's face was a ghastly gray-white, the eyes were lifeless and her pupils wide and unseeing. Electrical complexes flitted by in regular procession across the screen of the monitor at the head of the bed, gliding up and down on the oscilloscope with the rhythmic chest compression.

"OK, hold the CPR, please."

For that instant, it was quiet as all eyes looked to the monitor and the physician's fingers vainly sought again some sort of spontaneous blood movement in the vessels. The lurid light of the gray dawn crept into the room, like a specter that had arrived to claim the woman's soul. Gary felt a chill tingle up his spine as he looked at the lifeless body in front of him. Just a few more minutes of CPR, to circulate the drug that might break up the clot, he figured.

"If the tPA fails, then I'll call the arrest and pronounce her."

"Another bolus of epinephrine, and let's resume the chest compression. Do we have a potassium level back on that bloodwork? Or cardiac enzymes? What's her hemoglobin?"

150

A tray had been prepared, and he donned a gown and sterile gloves. Working quickly, he was able to locate the jugular vein with his large-bore needle, then threaded a wire into the vessel. Over this he placed a dilator, and removed it, following with the large "central" IV that would allow for quicker access of drugs to the central circulation. He taped it in place with sterile, transparent dressing, not bothering to sew it in. He figured she wouldn't actually have it for very long.

Julie blustered back into the room with several papers with lab results and carrying the tPA infusion. The nurses busily readied it for administration into the IV while emergency physician looked at the labs. They were all normal, or only slightly off. Nothing explained her present state. Gary hoped that the tPA might open up her pulmonary vessels and relieve the strain on her heart. But her vital organs had been so poorly perfused for such a long time that he was pessimistic. The cardiac muscle cells and her brain cells were probably irreversibly damaged. The two nurses took turns applying CPR to the patient as the "clot buster" drug infused. The chest rose and fell rhythmically under the nurses' hands, with each breath delivered by the respiratory therapist.

"I think I have a pulse," Gary called out excitedly as he palpated the neck. "Hold the CPR!"

The pulse rate had accelerated to 160, and a thready femoral pulse was now palpable. Lizzy cycled the automated blood pressure cuff.

"It's up to 95 over 60, doctor. Do you think it's just the epinephrine?"

"I think it's playing some role, Lizzy. God only knows if the tPA is helping. Keep infusing it, and keep the fluids and epi open. Maybe we'll get her to the ICU."

Struck suddenly with a note of optimism, Gary began to wonder if there was indeed a chance to save this woman. She'd had artificial circulation from CPR provided for her since the moment of her arrest. Maybe her brain and heart could survive this extraordinary insult, but he doubted it.

"The pressure's back down," commented Lizzy, a minute later, frowning. "I can't feel the pulse now."

"Damn," mumbled the physician, disgustedly. "OK, restart the CPR."

And so the resuscitation efforts continued, with brief periods of hope supervening whenever a pulse was palpable. But this lapsed into longer and longer intervals of pulselessness and despair on the part of the diminutive team that was ardently trying to rescue her. Each time blood coursed spontaneously through her arteries, artificial circulation was stopped, and there was renewed dedication to purpose, along with cautious optimism. Each time the pulsation disappeared, their hope would ebb away again. Fifteen minutes later, the emotionally wrenching episode came to a close as her feeble, aged heart collapsed, no longer able to respond to their pharmacologic ministrations. The thick, muscular walls were now exhausted and incapable of further coordinated contraction. The pulsations were gone, forever.

Gary hung his head and walked out slowly.

"6:48a.m.," he said, snapping his gloves off for emphasis. "Call the coroner, and see if they want to do a postmortem."

The next few minutes were spent completing the death certificate, and confirming for the coroner that this was unlikely to be foul play or some mysterious entity-just the death of an old lady from apparently natural causes. An autopsy would have been helpful to satisfy the physician's curiosity, but would be of little use to the patient's family. The coroner was very unlikely to pursue it.

Consumed by exhaustion and momentary despair, the emergency physician then collapsed heavily in his chair, and put his head in his hands. His weariness was evident in the sagging lines of his middle-aged face. Karen handed him the phone. The patient's primary care physician had called in, responding to their frantic pages of the prior few minutes. Gary explained what had transpired, and graciously received the thanks of the physician, who was hurrying off to his morning rounds. The PCP had the name of the patient's son, and would call him to break the bad news. Likely, he then faced a long day at the office, seeing dozens of sick patients.

7a.m.

"Not a moment too soon," Gary commented, as Terry Johnson, his relief for the day shift, entered the emergency department. The radio went off at exactly that moment.

With some satisfaction, Gary handed him the receiver.

Johnson nodded, took report and gave some orders.

"Chest pain, 70 years old, history of bypass, hypertension and heart failure. Probably someone you sent home last night," he joked.

His dry, incisive wit took some getting used to, but Gary

152

could only sigh.

"Maybe, Terry, maybe."

"What can I do to get you home this morning?"

Cocking his head, the physician thought for a moment. "There shouldn't be too much to do. Psych is evaluating a suicidal fellow with a history of substance abuse who wants to sign in. I think they'll accept him here. If not, hopefully at St. Francis. It's voluntary at this point. Back in room eight, there's an elderly woman who fell and probably has a proximal humerus fracture. I'm still waiting for films. She's pretty stoic- she'll need an ortho referral and she has a supportive daughter to care for her.

"Oh, and I have a lady in five that I tapped about an hour ago. The fluid was clear. She presented with fever, abdominal pain, UTI symptoms and a headache. She looked sick and her white count was elevated, so I worked her up out the wazoo, but everything is negative. Good news is, she feels better, the fever's down, her pain is gone and the headache got better after the tap- imagine! Clinically, she looks much better and if her CSF is normal, she can go home with symptomatic therapy and close follow up. It's probably a virus. I've written admit orders on an elderly guy with a GI bleed, and a lady in CHF-both going to ICU. There's another psych consult for a mentally disabled guy who needs placement, brought in by his brother because they can't care for him at home anymore. He's quite stable. The last psych situation is a man who OD'ed on heroin, and the medics gave him narcan. He was fine when he got here, but he's depressed and wants to arrange some sort of counseling. He's not suicidal, and I think he can be followed as an outpatient. His tox screen is pending, and Randall is about to go see him. He's a nice guy with a big problem. Pathetic situation, honestly."

"Aren't they all?" the other physician eyed him curiously, as though it was a waste to attach such sentimental statements to his report.

"Yeah, Terry. Pretty much. It's enough to make me depressed, too."

"Well, buck up. It's his problem. All you can do is try to help. Go get some sleep. You back tonight?"

"Unfortunately, yes. I hate Saturday nights. Too many drunks, too many fights."

"Yeah, and lately too many prisoners. That's one of the things that I really won't miss when they close this place."

"What do you mean?" Gary queried.

"They'll have to find someplace else to cater to the prison

153

population. If I never see an angry man with hepatitis in handcuffs get pushed into my exam room again, I'll be positively giddy."

Gary grunted his assent. "Will you be here tomorrow morning, too?" he asked.

"No, I've got the rest of the weekend off."

"Good for you, Terry-enjoy it." He turned to the nurses, busily involved in their own post-resuscitation paperwork, dutifully documenting every intervention and response.

"Lizzy, Maryann-see you tonight, Lord willing. I'm out of here."

"Yes, doctor. See you tonight for another round," Maryann called, cheerfully.

Lizzy was quiet and sullen. Unlike her co-worker, she required a much longer time to recover from the death of a patient. She would carry the tragedy home with her, a mantle of personal failure cloaked about her, as would Gary.

He ambled back to the call room, washed his face and grabbed his bag. His head ached from exhaustion but his thoughts ricocheted about inside his head. Sleep would be difficult, even more so than usual, on this day. At four, he'd be up for dinner, ready to start over again. Afterwards, he'd be tired, but in a strange, restless way that didn't require sleep. Then he'd be back in the ED again. Each night the fatigue became worse, until he was enervated from the very start of the shift. Only one more night and he'd be off of the overnight shift. Then, after two days of recuperation, he would be back to a more normal existence. He ached for the normalcy of the daytime routine and made his way back down to the main floor of the hospital, yearning to walk out into the bright morning light.

He paused for a moment, and turned about, walking into the hallway through which he'd passed the evening before. One of the maintenance men was making his way in for the day, and greeted the tired physician with a verve that startled Gary. Donna, from medical records, went bustling by with an armload of charts. Doctors, techs and nurses walked by briskly, chatting amiably as they sipped coffee purchased from the gift shop.

Gary once again looked upon the photos he'd studied the night before, from an era when the hospital had been focused almost solely upon providing care, with much less concern about a bottom line. Sadly, he reminded himself, institutions, like patients, served noble causes, aged, and died. The four walls, the bricks and mortar, the administrative structure, the devoted staff-

154

none could forestall the inevitable when a hospital had outlived its purpose in a society. He thought again of the cold, taught body which lay enshrouded one flight above, in the ED, and could not escape the comparison. Perhaps, he thought, the hospital would soon face its own demise. The great mills and furnaces had once been the engines for a city, a region, even a nation. They'd become rusting hulks, some collapsing, many long since demolished. The woman, the steel industry, the hospital. He tried to reconcile all of it, the enormous sense of loss, tried to gain perspective.

Retracing his route from the night before, he felt his lids sagging as he ascended the long grade to the top of the bluffs. Cresting the rise, he turned onto Grandview Avenue, the tourist route, with its exhilarating views of the city below, a city cradled in a valley and straddling three rivers, all knitted together by dozens of spindly bridges. He could not shake his despair, or his sense of inadequacy; too many bad things were happening at once. It was time. There were other avenues, other callings, other ways to matter. Across the river, he could make out the tiny figures moving briskly on the downtown sidewalks, hurrying into their office buildings, intent upon their respective destinations. Like ants in bustling colony, each had his own task, his own direction, his own contribution to the whole.

For Gary, the contribution was about to change. He would not slip gently under the waves with the dying hospital, nor bow and scrape to a massive bureaucracy that would likely toss him aside or infuriate him with its demands of assimilation. Weary, but resolute, his decision was made: he would not enter the ED again without beginning to undertake a pathway toward different field. If that required another year back in training, it was a price he was willing to pay. He thought of occupational medicine- bumps, bruises, twist, back pain, stomach aches, workplace safety assessments, all on a schedule- it seemed calm, and rewarding. He knew that there was an opportunity for just such a position in an emerging workplace health care service organization downtown. A smile spread across his face, and deep inside himself he felt a warm and curious sensation. He nodded. Yes, he could be an ant. And for the first time in many months, and perhaps years, Gary Phillips felt, but for a moment, a hint of satisfaction.

About the Author

Steven L. Orebaugh is an academic anesthesiologist at the University of Pittsburgh school of medicine. He received broad training in emergency medicine, critical care medicine and anesthesiology, and practiced in both the emergency department and the operating room until 2002, when he chose to devote all of his energies to anesthesiology. In addition, he served 20 years as a U.S. Navy medical officer, in both the active and reserve forces, retiring as a Captain in 2007. He is primarily interested in the subspecialty of regional anesthesia, instructing medical students, residents and fellows in this discipline, as well as carrying out research. He has written and edited several medical texts, and is the author of "Understanding Anesthesia," an informative book written for laypersons, to aid their comprehension of pain control in the modern surgical environment. Dr. Orebaugh lives in Western Pennsylvania, with his wife and daughter, and the family's three Yorkshire terriers.

47135661R00091

Made in the USA
Charleston, SC
03 October 2015